Cesca Adey studied for a degree in English Literature at the University of York and went on to work at film companies, art magazines and as a tutor to children before writing *Chloe*, her first novel. "I thought I could offer a unique perspective on children who are adopted or fostered," she says. "I was adopted myself at the age of seven, following long-term fostering, although *Chloe* is actually based on my experience of when my brother Michael was adopted. For a long time, I'd been the youngest child, so I was very excited when he came along." Cesca Adey grew up in Wiltshire but now lives in the USA.

Happy Birthday Kori!

Much Love

Cesca & Michael x

CHLOE

CESCA ADEY

WALKER BOOKS
AND SUBSIDIARIES
LONDON · BOSTON · SYDNEY · AUCKLAND

First published 2005 by Walker Books Ltd
87 Vauxhall Walk, London SE11 5HJ

2 4 6 8 10 9 7 5 3

Text © 2005 Cesca Adey
Cover illustration © 2005 Blaise Thompson

The right of Cesca Adey to be identified as author of this work has been asserted
by her in accordance with the Copyright, Designs and Patents Act 1988

This book has been typeset in Officina and Tree-Persimmon

Printed in Great Britain by Cox & Wyman Ltd, Reading, Berkshire

British Library Cataloguing in Publication Data:
a catalogue record for this book
is available from the British Library

ISBN 1-84428-942-7

www.walkerbooks.co.uk

*For my brother, Michael
– lots of love to you.
A little from both
our stories.*

CHAPTER ONE

I lay on my bed, staring up at the ceiling. Not that there was anything especially interesting up there, but then there wasn't anything especially interesting in the rest of my room either, except for the drawings and poems that I kept hidden under my bed. I didn't really care what the rest of my room looked like, though, as long as these things were in order. Of course, I had to make sure Mum and Dad didn't see them. I was a very private person – even if some people around here didn't appreciate that.

These weren't exactly turning out to be the best summer holidays ever. We had just moved house. Now we were living in the middle of nowhere. I didn't have a friend in at least a two-hundred-mile radius. It was all because of Gran. Mum was worried about her getting old and frail. She wanted to move closer to her, so we could keep an eye on things. Never mind that Gran was the biggest hypochondriac in the whole of the south of England. She had so many imaginary illnesses, it was sick.

I really wished I could go back up to Edinburgh. My life would be much better then. No doubt my friends were all having a great time without me. It wasn't fair, me being stuck here. I spent nearly all of my time in my bedroom, drawing pictures. I had done about twenty of my puppy, Hercules. I'd also done pictures of my clothes heaped on the floor, with the yellow wallpaper behind. Then there were the self-portraits. At first, I'd tried to make myself look really pretty. But that didn't last long. I was scowling in most of the pictures. I had all these variations of me with my messy brown hair (that some people called curly) and hazel-green eyes. I thought it was cool, the way my eyes changed colour depending on the light.

I planned to be a famous artist when I grew up. If that didn't work out, I had a backup plan. I would start my own sign-making company. I had been busy making signs for a while. I gave some away as presents, but most of them went up on my door. I liked to warn my parents: "Don't try knocking", "The world's most miserable teenager", "You'll be sorry", "No one understands" and "No, I won't come downstairs for dinner".

I had been in a bad mood for quite a while now. Mum called it my six-month marathon. It had actually started before we moved house. I hadn't been as happy in Edinburgh as I liked to tell myself. Mum said thirteen was a difficult age. But it was more than that. I had started feeling different to other people. I wondered if it had something to do with being adopted.

My past seemed very mysterious. I had only lived with Mum and Dad since I was four. I couldn't remember much before then. Apparently, I'd lived with foster families. I also lived with my natural mum for a year after I was born, but she couldn't look after me. No one seemed to know who my natural dad was. I didn't really mind so much about that. It was more my natural mum I thought about.

Sometimes I looked at strangers on the street

and wondered if I could be related to them. I especially looked for people who were tall and skinny, like me. But that could have been just about anyone. I sometimes felt tempted to tap people on the shoulder and ask if they were missing a little girl called Chloe Tulip (who wasn't quite so little any more). Of course, I never actually did this.

Mum and Dad said they were happy to talk about my past any time I wanted. But that didn't really appeal to me. I tended not to open up to them very much. I kept a lot of things to myself. Anyway, what could they tell me? They might have a few extra facts I didn't already know, but I had more than enough imagination.

I liked to make up stories about my natural mum. In one of them, she was a poor poet who lived in a flat without electricity. She really wanted to keep me, but she didn't have enough money and social services took me away. This left her with a broken heart and she dreamed of finding me again.

In another story, she was a movie star. She had loads of money and drove expensive cars. She had everything, but she wasn't happy. There was a big tragedy in her life: her daughter had been stolen from her. She searched everywhere and hired private detectives, but she never found her.

True stories weren't quite so exciting. I looked out of my window at the thatched cottages opposite and the fields stretching into the distance. It was so boring here. BORING! It didn't matter how loudly I said it because no one could hear me. I had my bedroom door shut (as always). Hercules was lying on the floor next to me, chewing an old teddy bear.

"Well, at least I've got you," I said, stroking his ears.

He thumped his tail against the carpet. He was the best dog ever. He wouldn't win any dog shows (even though he had a beauty spot by his nose, like Marilyn Monroe!) but he had loads of personality and he liked to race around whenever he got the chance. He was my only friend in Little Meadows.

What kind of a name was Little Meadows, anyway? It sounded like we were living in a field (which I guess we pretty much were). Mum had told me that a thousand people lived in the village, but I hadn't seen them. I had spent hours looking out of my window over the last few weeks. So far, I had spotted the occasional man walking a dog, the odd family strolling by. The only other signs of life were the white ducks waddling along to the village pond.

When I'd lived in Edinburgh, I used to stay in my room quite often, but not as much as I did now. There had always been a lot going on there. And we'd had noise: ambulance sirens, rush-hour traffic. I couldn't get used to all this quiet. It was giving me a headache.

Things weren't so quiet at Grandma Kettle's house though: she never stopped talking. She also drank more tea than anyone I had ever met. And this wasn't normal tea: it was a tar-black brew. She would put about ten tea bags in the pot and leave them to steep for hours.

I didn't exactly volunteer to go over for visits. I'd be ordered to go round and search for things that had gone missing. Gran was always losing things – though I suspect she was really just after my company.

I was very much in demand these days – only not with anyone I wanted to be around. Mum and

Dad were always trying to get me to leave my room. In the evenings, they would suggest I came downstairs to watch TV with them. I had to make it clear: I was a busy person; I couldn't spend my evenings in front of the TV. If I was going to be famous one day, I had a lot of creating to do. In other words, I would wait until Mum and Dad had gone to bed, then I'd go and watch TV. That way, I got the whole house to myself, which made much better sense.

My parents and I kept very different hours: they got up at dawn; I got up at noon. And I have to say, they weren't always the most considerate people. They would make a racket first thing in the morning and wake me up. They were always calling upstairs or moving the car or inviting people over. And they wondered why I was so moody.

I told myself to stop thinking about everything so much. All I seemed to do these days was think, think, think. I got off my bed and looked at the calendar. I had another thirty-two days, eleven hours and twenty-eight minutes of the summer holidays left. I wondered what I was going to do with all that time.

Just then, Mum started calling, "Chloe! Chloe!"

"What is it?" I shouted back.

"Can you come downstairs, please? We have important news."

Important news? I hoped I wasn't going to be sent over to Gran's to look for something else she'd "lost". Or that Mum wasn't about to give me the latest list of chores: clean your room, bring down your dirty washing, empty the dishwasher... Or maybe we were moving back up to Edinburgh!

Hercules went over to the door, wagging his tail.

"Come on," I said. "Let's find out what this is all about."

CHAPTER TWO

When I got downstairs, I found Mum and Dad in the kitchen. They were looking very happy about something. Dad even had a plate of his home-made biscuits out.

"Dad's been cooking again," Mum said.

"So I see," I replied.

"Help yourself," he said. "They're white choco-late and almond."

I took the biscuit with the most chocolate in it and broke some off for Hercules, who was lying under the table.

"I'm thinking of making honey and walnut bread next," Dad went on.

One thing I wanted to try to avoid was an end-less conversation about nothing in particular (what

Mum called a pleasant chat). I hadn't come down-stairs to be sociable. I needed to find out what was going on.

"So, what's the important news?" I asked.

Mum and Dad glanced at each other.

"You know how we've been looking into adopt-ing another child," Dad began.

I nodded, reluctantly. They'd been talking about it for years, though nothing had ever come of it.

"Well, we finally have some good news. We've found a brother for you!" Mum said.

I almost choked on my biscuit. Mum had to come and pat my back.

"You're joking," I spluttered.

"Isn't it wonderful," Dad said.

He didn't seem to have noticed me almost dying across the table from him.

"We're so lucky to have found Ollie," he contin-ued.

Mum squeezed his arm to let him know there was a problem. A BIG problem.

"What's wrong, Chloe?" she asked.

"You can't just suddenly say you're adopting someone else," I told her.

"But we've been talking about adopting another child for a long time. And we have talked to you about Ollie before," Mum said.

I tried to remember. A while ago, they might have mentioned something about going to visit him. But that wasn't the same as actually going ahead and adopting him.

I thought I'd better just make things clear to them.

"I don't want a brother," I said.

"You always said you wanted one before," Dad replied.

"I've changed my mind."

"Ollie is the sweetest little two-year-old."

"I'm sure some other family would love to have him then," I said.

I knew I was being mean, but I'd really had enough. First Mum and Dad had made me move to Little Meadows – and now this.

"We thought you'd be happy," Dad said.

"That only shows how little you know me," I replied.

I ran out of the kitchen, slamming the door behind me as hard as I could, and ran upstairs to my room. I got out my special sign – the one I used for emergencies – and put it on my door. It read: "EXPLOSIONS! Keep clear!" Then I lay down on my bed. At least my parents wouldn't disturb me now (no more than they already had).

I started daydreaming about my natural mum. Maybe she would come and get me. Then I wouldn't have to deal with my parents any more. She'd take me away from Little Meadows in her limo. We'd go up to Edinburgh and live in a big house. I wouldn't ever have to come back here again.

There was a knock on my door.

"Chloe," Mum said, "can we come in?"

"Read the sign," I replied.

I hadn't put it there for fun. But Mum and Dad didn't pay any attention to the explosions warning. They let themselves in. I couldn't stand them being here, invading my space. My room was meant to be private.

Mum perched on the end of my bed, while Dad cleared the clothes off my chair and sat down. I shuffled closer to the wall, trying to keep my distance.

"I'm sorry you're upset," Mum said.

"I'm fine," I replied.

In other words, I didn't want to talk about it.

"You've had a lot of changes in your life lately," Mum continued.

"Way too many," I muttered.

"But you'll soon get used to things here."

"You and Ollie are going to get along really well," Dad said.

"Don't bet on it."

"You know, you and Ollie have a lot in common. You both had a difficult time before you were adopted," Mum said.

I really resented her saying that. I thought desperately of my natural mum and how she was going to come for me one day, pulling up in front of the house in her limo...

"Chloe?" Mum said, looking worried.

My natural mum probably never wanted me to be adopted in the first place. It was all a big mistake.

I wanted to get out of there and be by myself. I got off my bed and stumbled over to the door, trying not to trip over the stuff Dad had piled on the floor. Then I turned towards my parents. I felt like crying, but instead I started shouting.

"I wish I'd never been adopted," I yelled. "You stole me from my real mum. I would have been much better off staying with her. All you want to do is ruin my life!"

CHAPTER THREE

I felt really bad. I shouldn't have said those things. And I shouldn't have stormed out of the room. I just got so worked up sometimes. And those thoughts about my natural mum were silly. I knew she wasn't really going to show up here. She probably didn't even care about me.

Part of me wanted to say sorry to Mum and Dad. But they were the ones who'd started it all by talking about adopting someone else. I wondered what was so great about Ollie. Why did they like him so much? He was probably really well-behaved all the time. I bet he wouldn't be rude and moody like me.

Maybe my parents were doing this to get back at me for my six-month bad mood. Mum did keep saying it was about time I snapped out of it. Adopting Ollie might be their way of punishing me. Or maybe I was getting too old and too difficult, and he was meant as some sort of replacement. Mum and Dad didn't want me any more. They wanted to start again with Ollie.

I tried to work out how long it would be until Ollie moved in. A day? A week? A year? I could plan what to do when he lived here. I had already got into practice by shutting myself in my room a lot. I could actually just live in my room when the time came. That way, I'd have nothing to do with him. I could forget he existed. Hercules would still be my friend and there was always Grandma Kettle to talk to, if I ever got really desperate for company.

I went outside. I didn't feel like being in the house any more. I looked around at the mini-jungle of weeds. The garden needed some serious work. Hercules was busy chewing a stick, but he came bounding over when he saw me, almost knocking me flat.

"I don't know what to do about all this," I said, bending down to stroke him.

Hercules slobbered on the side of my face and I had to push him away. I threw a stick for him to chase.

I walked over to the fence. There was a small clearing in the bushes, where Mum and Dad wouldn't be able to see me. I could stay hidden for a while. Hopefully Hercules wouldn't give me away. He was already running back. He dropped the stick at my feet, but I wasn't going to keep throwing it for him again and again.

"Lie down," I said.

He didn't take any notice. I patted the ground and he tried to lick my hand. Finally I gave up. He could do whatever he wanted.

Then I got a shock.

"Nice dog," said a voice behind me.

I turned around and saw a girl of about my age looking over the fence. She had short brown hair and blue eyes. She looked friendly and a little mischievous at the same time.

"I'm Kate, by the way," she said.

"Hi, I'm Chloe and this is Hercules."

Hercules wagged his tail frantically as Kate reached over to stroke him.

"Have you and your family just moved in?" she asked.

"A few weeks ago."

"I haven't seen you around the place."

"I've been quite busy," I said vaguely.

"I heard you're related to Mrs Kettle," she said.

I nodded. "She's my gran."

"She must be really happy that you're here," she said.

"I suppose," I replied.

"Angie told me she used to be ever so depressed."

"What do you mean?" I asked.

"She hardly ever left her house. Angie used to do meals-on-wheels and she often found her sitting alone in the dark. But these last few weeks she's been like a different person."

I found it strange to think of Grandma Kettle sitting in the dark. She was always so full of life when I saw her, clearing everyone out of the way with her walking stick or poisoning people with her tar-black tea.

"So, who's Angie?" I asked.

"My foster mum," Kate replied. "I moved in with her a few years ago. We get along pretty well most of the time. We're more like friends really."

"I thought I'd be the only one around here with a weird family history," I said.

"In what way?" Kate asked.

"I was adopted when I was four," I replied.

I paused. There was something about Kate that made me trust her. She was very open and friendly. Also, she was fostered, so she'd probably understand what I was going through. I decided to tell her about Ollie.

"My parents have just told me they're adopting another child," I said.

"I thought you seemed upset," she replied.

"It was bad enough having to move house, let alone having a two-year-old boy come here as well."

"You might end up really liking him," Kate said.

"I doubt that very much."

I heard Hercules barking. Suddenly I thought that my parents could still be in my room. I was afraid Mum might have started one of her major cleaning operations (the kind when she "accidentally" read a load of my poems and looked through my drawings, then a few days later there was one framed in the living-room).

"I'd better go," I said.

"Come round to my house any time you want," Kate replied.

I waved and hurried inside. When I got upstairs, my room was empty and it didn't look like my parents had been going through my things. I sat down on my bed, feeling relieved. Now I'd talked to Kate I definitely felt better than before. I might even have made a new friend! Maybe things weren't going to be so bad after all.

CHAPTER FOUR

The next morning, I woke to the sound of banging and crashing. It was coming from the spare room. With sleep-blurred eyes, I looked over at my clock: 11.24 a.m. It was early morning, for goodness' sake! My parents knew I didn't get up until twelve at the earliest. And they had to go making such a racket.

I'd been up late the night before. I'd watched TV and shared some mint chocolate chip ice cream with Hercules. I was surprised he liked that flavour so much. It was a favourite of mine too. The last thing I felt like doing right then was getting out of bed. But I did.

I had to go and tell Mum and Dad what I thought about all the noise. As I shuffled down the hallway, I was building up a speech in my head about how not everyone woke up at the crack of dawn like them.

Then I heard Mum say, "Hercules was sick quite a few times this morning. Maybe I should take him to the vet."

"It must be something he ate," Dad replied. "He's always digging things up in the garden."

"It didn't look much like anything from the garden to me," Mum said.

At a guess, I'd have said it probably looked more like something from the freezer: that mint chocolate chip ice cream. But I wasn't saying anything.

I had this sudden genius plan to disappear back to my room. But then Dad walked out of the spare room.

"Morning, Chloe," he said.

"Morning," I mumbled.

"Isn't it a bit early for you to be awake?"

"Now you mention it, I was about to complain about all the noise."

"Sorry, love," Dad said. "We're just trying to clear out the spare room for Ollie."

"He's not moving in already, is he?" I asked, getting worried.

"Not for another week or two," Dad replied.

I went back into my room and shut the door. I couldn't believe it was really happening: Ollie was moving in. He had his own room. He was taking over the house. I had to do something.

I got dressed and then I had a quick peek out into the hallway. There was no one there so I went over to the stairs. I had a good view into the spare room. It didn't look like much furniture was left. Dad was opening a can of yellow paint. Mum had the vacuum cleaner going. It was making this loud roaring noise. I could swear that thing had sucked away half my decent clothes. Mum liked to come into my room sometimes and vacuum up everything in sight.

Hercules came over and lay down on my feet.

"My own personal foot warmer," I said.

He wasn't paying any attention. He'd rolled over and was biting at my shoelaces. He must have decided they looked like good chewing material. Hercules kept a whole store of chewed-up things behind his basket – mainly teddies but also the odd shoe, slipper, stick, chewed-up tissue. He wasn't too fussy. He must have thought that no one knew about it and he was always secretly adding stuff to his collection.

I tried to imagine what it would be like when Ollie was actually in that room. What if he cried all the time? I'd have *him* messing up my sleep, as well as my parents. There had been a time when I would have loved to have a brother or a sister. I still liked the idea of having someone who needed me and looked up to me. But he'd just get in my way all the time. He'd be another person who didn't pay attention to what my signs said and let himself into my room whenever he felt like it.

Mum emerged from the spare room.

"Why don't you come and help, Chloe?" she asked.

"I'm busy right now."

"Doing what?"

"Stuff."

Mum looked at Hercules tugging away at my shoelaces.

"You could take Hercules for a walk," she said. "It'd be better than lurking."

What was it with Mum? She had this really annoying way of saying things. "Lurking" was completely the wrong description. I wasn't lurking. I was subtly estimating the strength of the enemy from a distance. But that seemed like a bit of a mouthful to say all at once.

I felt myself getting angry again. I kept thinking about how I wasn't really appreciated. Mum obviously wanted to get rid of me. Why else would she tell me to go for a walk? Maybe it'd be better if I left for good. There were plenty of places I could go. I let myself out through the front door and set off down the road with Hercules. Mum and Dad would be sorry for treating me so badly.

The road out of the village curved up a steep hill. My anger got me about halfway up, but then I was exhausted. My body wasn't used to such sudden bursts of exercise.

"It's hard work running away," I told Hercules.

He didn't seem at all fazed by the climb. But he did want to go back down the hill and chase ducks at the village pond. I had to hold him back by his collar.

"That's the wrong direction," I said. "We're trying to get out of this place."

I sat down on the grassy bank and looked up

the hill. There was a clear line on the horizon where the road met the blue sky. There had to be easier methods of running away than this. In films, people didn't have this problem – they just stuck out their thumb and hitched a lift to wherever they were going.

I thought I might try and hitchhike up to Edinburgh. At least I knew a few people there. I could stay with some of my friends. I went over to the side of the road and stuck out my thumb.

CHAPTER FIVE

After a while, a car slowed down. I began to lose my nerve. Did I really want to go all the way back up to Edinburgh? I hadn't even brought any extra clothes. Mum and Dad would phone the police and report me missing, then I'd be in trouble. I checked in my pocket. I only had about a pound. I wasn't going to get anywhere with that. How would I feed Hercules?

Running away didn't seem like such a great idea any more. The car stopped next to me and a man rolled down the window.

"Where are you going?" he asked.

"Nowhere. Don't worry."

I backed away from the car and started walking down the hill. I kicked a stone along the ground as I went. I still didn't want to go home. But where else was there? I felt trapped. I didn't especially want to go to Gran's house. She would probably make me look for her hearing aid, or something. Ever since she'd got one for her imaginary deafness, she could never find it. Dad said that she lost it deliberately so she could pick and choose what she heard.

I thought about going to Kate's house. She seemed like a cool person and she'd said I could stop by. But then, she might not have meant it. She probably had loads of other friends.

While I was still trying to make up my mind, Hercules had a go at chasing the ducks in the village pond. Some old ladies waiting at the bus stop frowned at me and told me off for not keeping him under control. So I pulled him out of the pond. He had green stuff hanging from him and he was dripping wet.

This wasn't ideal for visiting someone I hardly knew. But I decided I might as well. I made my way over to Kate's house and knocked on the door. A woman answered.

"You must be Chloe," she said, with a smile.

"I've heard all about you. I'm Angie. Come in. I'll go and find Kate for you."

I looked guiltily at Hercules.

"He's a bit wet," I said.

"No problem," she replied.

She put some newspaper on the floor. Luckily Hercules was exhausted by now. He lay down quietly.

Angie went over to the stairs and called, "Kate! You'll never guess who's here."

Kate came downstairs.

"Brilliant," she said. "I was hoping you'd come by."

We went into the kitchen and Kate poured out two glasses of lemonade from the fridge.

"So, how's it all going?" she asked.

I hadn't really been planning to tell Kate what had been going on, but she seemed genuinely interested and it was a relief to have someone to talk to.

"My parents are being a real nightmare," I began. "They've been getting Ollie's room ready for him. I don't know why they want to adopt someone else. Aren't I good enough for them?"

"I'm sure that's not it," Kate replied. "Have you talked to them about it?"

"They're impossible to talk to. At the moment, I just want to be as far away from them as possible. I thought about running away just now, but I didn't get very far."

"I've done that a few times myself," Kate said.

"I didn't even make it to the top of the hill," I said.

"You will with practice," Kate replied.

I found myself smiling for what seemed like the first time in ages. Kate was so nice and I felt I could really talk to her.

After we'd chatted for a while, I checked on Hercules. He was sleeping on the newspapers. He looked a lot drier. I thought about going home. My parents were probably really worried. They'd be searching all over the village by now.

"I'd better go and let my parents know I'm alive," I said.

"I think you've given them enough time to get worried," Kate said.

"I hope so," I replied.

CHAPTER SIX

When I got home, no one even seemed to have noticed I'd gone. Mum and Dad were standing by the front door with Grandma Kettle.

"Why don't we all go into the kitchen," Mum suggested.

Gran led the way, pushing open doors with her walking stick. Then she sat herself at the head of the table.

Mum put the kettle on.

"Oh, good," Gran said. "I was hoping for some tea. An old lady can't go without her tea."

She certainly couldn't.

Dad got this excited look on his face. He went over to the cupboard and pulled out about twenty boxes of tea. They were all different flavours.

He had done a special shop at the supermarket to get them. He was trying to win Gran over, hoping that, after eighteen years, she might finally accept him as her son-in-law.

Gran didn't even seem to see the boxes of tea being piled up in front of her. Maybe she was having an attack of imaginary blindness now.

"Look, Gran," I said.

"At what, dear?" she asked.

"I bought you all these teas," said Dad. "There's orange flavour, lemon, peach and raspberry, green tea..."

Gran turned to Mum.

"I'm surprised you allow this," she said. "All this voodoo and foreign matter on your table. I certainly wouldn't."

"But you love tea," Mum replied.

"I love proper tea, yes. But not all this. This herbal stuff makes a mockery of the real thing. I'm sure the Honourable Cedric Hamilton wouldn't have approved. You should have married him, like I told you to."

"Don't go on about that again," Mum said.

Gran sat back in her chair.

"You could have lived in a mansion by Windy Woods. The biggest house for miles around – and you turned it all down."

Gran always enjoyed it when she got to talk about the Honourable Cedric Hamilton. I could see her looking at Dad out of the corner of her eye. She liked to try and get a reaction out of him. But he had heard it so many times before that he carried on the same as usual.

I felt a bit sorry for him, especially after he'd gone to all that trouble.

"The peppermint tea tastes good," I said.

Gran patted my arm.

"Don't worry, dear," she replied. "I brought my own. I wouldn't leave home without it."

With that, she started rummaging in her tweed handbag. She brought out a handful of dusty tea bags.

"These will do for my cup," she said.

It took a long time to get Gran to leave. In the end, I offered to walk her home. She took my arm and hobbled along.

"Isn't it exciting about Ollie," she said.

"Thrilling," I replied.

"This must be a dream come true for you."

I wouldn't have put it that way exactly. But I didn't feel like arguing.

Gran only lived a couple of doors down from us, so it wasn't a long walk. We went through the gate with the sign I'd made for her last Christmas: "Trespassers will be severely beaten with a walking-stick."

"It's the best home security system I've ever had," she said.

She got out her keys and unlocked the door. I remembered what Kate had said about how Gran used to shut herself away a lot and sit in the dark.

"Are you going to be OK?" I asked.

She patted me on the arm and gave me a warm, wrinkled smile.

"I'm so glad to have you here," she said.

I helped her up the step into her house. Then I headed back. At the gate, I turned around and saw Gran still standing in the doorway, doing her royal wave. She certainly did seem happy.

At home, I found Dad busy inventing another of his recipes: a spicy orange sauce to go with roast duck (not from the village pond). It smelt good. I thought I might be helpful for a change and set the table. Mum came downstairs and admired what a fine job we were doing.

"I think the table looks especially good," I pointed out (I wanted to make sure I got full credit for my efforts).

Dad served the dinner and we sat down. I was hoping to eat my meal in peace, but Mum and Dad had other plans.

"You had us worried, running off earlier," Mum said.

So worried that they hadn't even bothered looking for me. But at least they'd noticed.

"Are you still upset about Ollie?" Dad asked.

"I just don't want to be around when he moves in," I replied.

"You could at least give him a chance. Imagine what it'll be like for him. He'll be in a completely new place, surrounded by strangers. He'll need all the help he can get settling in."

"Your mum's right, Chloe," Dad said. "We've been talking about it and we think it'd be good for you to meet Ollie before he comes here.

So we've arranged to visit him at his foster family's house. And we want you to come too."

CHAPTER SEVEN

I didn't want to go on this visit. All I wanted was to be left in peace, but Mum kept on at me.

"Chloe, time to get up."

I pulled my duvet over my head and tried to ignore her.

"Chloe..."

"OK, I'm getting up!" I shouted.

I threw on some of my scruffiest clothes. There was a shirt with holes in the elbows that I knew Mum especially disliked. I also put on my purple jeans – the ones I hid in different places around my room to stop Mum getting hold of them (I was afraid she'd put them in the washing machine and wash out all the colour).

Mum was shocked when she saw me.

"Go and get changed, right now," she said. "You can't go out looking like that."

"Like what?"

"Like you don't have anything nice to wear."

I wasn't the only person Mum was annoyed with.

"Your jumper's full of holes," she told Dad.

"My 'holy' jumper," he replied.

"What am I going to do with you two?" Mum said, with a sigh.

"Leave us alone?" I suggested.

Before we left, I took Hercules out for a run. He went chasing after a pigeon that had made the mistake of landing in the garden. I thought about what was going on. I had been dreading this whole trip. But, deep down, I wanted to find out what Ollie was like.

It was strange: only about a year ago, this would have been really exciting. I used to dream about what it would be like seeing my new brother or sister for the first time. But now it was actually happening, I was worried.

The pigeon escaped, only losing one feather, which was left dancing in the air. I wondered how

Hercules would react to having a little boy around the place. He liked to charge around like he was completely crazy, but he could also be quite gentle at times.

"Time to go!" Mum called.

"I'm not coming!" I shouted. "Hercules wants me to stay here with him. Don't you, Hercules?"

He licked my hand.

"Don't start this now – you'll make us late," Mum said.

"Good," I muttered.

I took Hercules back inside, then trudged over to the car.

Dad was already there, sitting in the passenger seat with his enormous book on the Scottish Highlands open on his lap. That thing looked like it weighed a ton; it must have had about a million chapters. He was leaning over it, his glasses balanced on the end of his nose.

"Hello there, Chloe," he said as I climbed in.

I crossed my arms firmly and stared out of the window. I didn't feel much like talking to anyone, not after being dragged out of bed so early in the morning.

"I don't want to go," I said and kicked the seat in front to make it clear how unhappy I was.

"This is important. You're going to meet Ollie."

"I can't wait."

"He's a wonderful little boy."

"If he's so great, then why don't his foster family want to keep him?"

"I think they wanted to, but..."

Mum arrived with the car keys jingling. She got behind the steering wheel and we set off. I forgot what Dad had been saying and put my headphones on to avoid any more conversation.

It took ages getting to Bridgewater – or Watering Bridge or Water-under-the-Bridge, whatever it was called. Finally we pulled up in front of a small terraced house. I saw the curtains at the downstairs window move, and a little face looked out. That must be Ollie, I thought. He disappeared again.

I followed my parents to the door.

"Are we all ready then?" Mum asked.

I quickly tied my hair back, in a last-minute effort to look more presentable.

Mum was about to knock, when a woman opened the door.

"Hello," she said. "Good to see you."

I shuffled in, trying to stay behind Mum. I was hoping no one would notice me and ask annoying questions.

"No hiding," Mum whispered.

"I'm not."

"This is Chloe," Mum told the woman.

"Hello, Chloe. I'm Jane," she replied. "From social services."

She had a very direct way of looking at people. I fidgeted under her gaze and mumbled something that I hoped would sound like a greeting.

I looked around for Ollie. He was sitting with his foster mum on the sofa. He had light reddish hair and big blue eyes, and he was clutching a little white cloth. I noticed he had a troubled expression. It was hard to describe exactly. It was like someone who had been hurt before understanding what that meant. It reminded me of photos of myself when I was his age.

Ollie's foster mum seemed to really care about him. She was obviously in no rush to give him to another family. She put some building blocks out on the floor for him to play with.

"Maybe Chloe will help you," she said.

I even considered it for a moment. But then Mum and Dad came over and started making a massive fuss of Ollie. Every little thing he did, they acted like it was the greatest thing in the world.

"He might be a builder when he's older," Dad said, when Ollie managed to put one building block on top of another.

We ended up going for a walk to the playground. I wasn't in a very good mood by this point. I took my time while the others walked on ahead of me, up the hill. Mum was holding Ollie's hand. I didn't see why that was necessary.

"Come on, Chloe," she called.

The others looked back at me.

"I'll catch you up," I said.

I watched them go over to the swings. I sat down on a bench, pretending to have nothing to do with them. I looked down at my shoes and focused on kicking wood chippings over to the fence. I wished I was anywhere but there. If only my natural mum would come for me, then I wouldn't have to deal with my family any more. She would take me away

in her limo. I would be the most special person in
the world to her.

CHAPTER EIGHT

Mum started having a go at me as soon as we got in the car.

"You could have made more of an effort with Ollie," she told me.

Then she said to Dad, "Why don't you tell her she should have made more of an effort?"

"She can work it out for herself," Dad said, and he went back to reading his book.

"You didn't need to sulk the whole time," Mum told me.

"I didn't sulk," I muttered.

"Pardon?" Mum asked.

"My real mum wouldn't have put me through all this. I wish I'd stayed with her."

I quickly pulled my headphones out of my bag

and started listening to some music. I heard Mum's voice pattering in the distance, but I ignored her and she gave up after a while.

I kept on telling myself I was right to be annoyed – that way I didn't have to think about hurting Mum's feelings. I decided to run away again – properly this time. I went through the things that I would need to pack: my drawings, a whole load of clothes and some posters. Also I would need to find the poems I had hidden around my room (to stop anyone reading them). I needed to be ready to go.

I wiped away a tear from the corner of my eye. There was nothing to be sad about. If I ran away, I'd escape having to deal with Ollie moving in. I'd told my parents that I didn't want a brother, but they hadn't listened to me. It wasn't my fault. A whole day of my summer holidays had been wasted going on that visit. I had done more than enough. Mum and Dad couldn't make me care about Ollie.

As soon as we got back, I headed straight up to my room. I put one of my signs up on the door: "Go Away!" Then I started collecting up my draw-ings and stuffing them into a bag. But I soon felt too depressed to do any more. I lay down on my bed, burying my head under my pillow. I didn't even want to hear my own thoughts.

There was a knock at the door.

"Chloe," Mum said.

"What?" I asked.

Mum ignored my sign (again). She let herself in, climbing over the heaps of stuff on the floor, and sat down next to me.

"I think we need to talk," she said.

She could talk all she wanted, as long as she didn't expect me to say anything.

"You seem confused about your biological mother," she continued.

I stayed silent.

"We've talked about this before. You know she's not some heroine who will take you away from your worries and make everything better. You were put up for adoption because she wasn't able to look after you."

I suddenly felt curious.

"What was wrong with her?" I asked.

There was a pause while Mum tried to work out what to say.

"She had problems with drugs," she said at last. "She kept leaving you places. I'm sure she didn't really mean to hurt you, but she wasn't acting in a responsible way."

"What else?"

I knew Mum was holding back.

"Once she left you alone in her flat for two days. Luckily the neighbours heard you crying and called the police. They got you out."

Mum put an arm around my shoulders.

"She didn't mean to leave me," I said.

"Of course not. She just wasn't very well."

"She loved me."

Mum didn't answer that.

"The one thing you need to remember is that Dad and I love you very much. It was the most exciting day of my life when we found out we were adopting you."

"Really?" I asked.

She nodded.

"We only had a few weeks to get ready. We rushed around, buying everything we thought you might need. Grandma Kettle kept coming over for extended cups of tea to find out more about you."

"What was I like when I first arrived?"

"You seemed very uncertain about everything. You didn't like to be left by yourself, especially at night."

"It's a bit different now."

"Yes," she said, smiling. "There weren't any midnight feasts with Hercules, sharing mint chocolate chip ice cream."

"How did you know?"

"It doesn't take Einstein to put two and two together: Hercules is sick, then the next day Dad is wondering where all the ice cream has gone..."

I was surprised she hadn't told me off about that.

"But seriously," she said, "you should give Ollie a chance. He's had a hard start in life, just like you did. His biological father used to hit him and put cigarettes out on him – all kinds of horrible things. Ollie ended up in hospital several times."

I was stunned. How could someone do that to a little boy?

"What about his natural mum?" I asked.

"She was very young when she had him. She wasn't really ready to have children. She looked after Ollie for a year and a half, or tried to."

"She couldn't stop him from being hurt?"

"Apparently not. But she did agree to social services putting him up for adoption. Maybe that was the best thing she could do for him."

CHAPTER NINE

Two weeks later, Ollie arrived. I was up in my room, watching from the window. Mum and Dad kept trying to get me to go downstairs.

"Why don't you come and wait with us?" Mum called.

"No, thanks," I replied.

Finally I saw a blue car pull up in front of the house. The social worker, Jane, got out. She took Ollie from the back seat. He was wearing a puffy jacket with a Superman T-shirt underneath, and he was holding on to his cloth. He had no idea that he was coming to his new home and that we were meant to be his family now.

Jane carried Ollie towards the house. Hercules went running over. He was trying to take hold of

Ollie's cloth (he probably thought it was something else for him to chew up). Mum and Dad went outside. Mum took Ollie – she looked thrilled. Dad was smiling a lot too. I couldn't help feeling left out, all alone in my room. Then Jane glanced up at my window.

I jumped on to my bed, out of sight. I reminded myself that I didn't want anything to do with the Ollie greeting party. There was no need for me to go downstairs. Ollie had enough attention with Mum and Dad hugging him and making a fuss.

I could hear voices at the bottom of the stairs. Jane was probably wondering why I was in my room. She'd think I was an awful person for not even coming down to say hi to Ollie. Of course, Mum had already given me a long list of reasons to feel sorry for him. But I wasn't going to feel sorry for anyone (except myself). I mean, I did think it was horrible that his natural dad used to beat him up and I knew it wasn't easy moving in with a new family, but it'd take more than that to make me like him.

My bedroom door opened. I couldn't see anyone there, so I sat up. Then I spotted Ollie.

"You must be my new brother," I said.

He had a puzzled expression on his face.

"How did you get up here?" I asked.

Jane popped her head around the door.

"Don't mind us," she said. "We're just having a quick look around the place."

"Chloe's room is usually out of bounds," I heard Mum say.

"That's right," I replied.

And I hadn't tidied it for the occasion either.

"Why don't you join us?" Dad suggested.

"I'm sort of busy at the moment," I replied.

"Oh," he said.

He sounded hurt. I thought I might as well go with them, but I wasn't going to tell them straight out. I waited until they had all left my room, then I climbed off my bed and followed.

They went into Ollie's room. There was still a faint smell of paint and dust in there. Ollie's bags were piled on the floor. He didn't seem to have much, but there were lots of teddies. An enormous cat with one eye was propped up against the bags; it was the kind of thing you win at the fair.

"So, you decided to come," Dad said, smiling.

I shrugged.

"I knew you wanted to really," he said.

He didn't need to make such a big deal out of it.

"The room looks lovely," Jane commented.

"We put a lot of work into it," Mum said.

When we left, Ollie wanted to bring along the giant cat. He tried to drag it out of the room.

"You can play with that later," Mum said.

"Hercules might steal it," I added.

"We don't want that to happen," Mum went on. She took the giant cat and propped it up by the window. "He can look after things up here."

We went downstairs, past the portrait of Gran's brother, Great-uncle Herbert. Gran had given it to my parents as a wedding present. "So you'll have someone to watch over you," she'd told them. Mum and Dad didn't really want anyone watching over them, so he had stayed in the attic while we were living in Edinburgh. But now we were pretty much next door to Gran, they felt obliged to hang the portrait somewhere.

Great-uncle Herbert had given me a fright quite a few times. When I passed by him in the night, on my way down to the kitchen for a snack, I would get the feeling that someone was there and it would be him, peering from the shadows. Then I'd have to sprint down to the kitchen and turn on the lights.

I never knew Great-uncle Herbert when he was alive, but, as a portrait, he looked very odd. He was painted in brown and white. His hair looked like a wig stuck on top of his head. His chin sank into his neck and his eyes were slightly crossed. For some reason, Grandma Kettle thought this picture was a masterpiece of the twentieth century.

I heard Mum explain to Jane, "It was a gift."

"He looks like quite a character," she said.

"Just like the person who gave it to us," Dad added.

"What do you think?" I asked Ollie.

He hid his face behind his cloth.

"Pretty scary, right?"

Dad wanted to go outside and show off the garden. Jane looked slightly bemused. There were weeds the same height as her.

"I'm thinking of growing yellow roses along the fence," Dad said. "I had a dream about it last night."

"Did that dream include mowing the grass?" Mum asked. "That would be the best place to start."

Ollie wandered off to look at the hose, which ran along the side of the house. Dad turned the tap on and Ollie was fascinated by the water that poured out. Hercules appeared from behind some of the weeds, where he had obviously been digging things up (his paws were really muddy). He ran over to the hose, crouched down and barked at the water. Ollie clapped his hands and Hercules barked even more.

Then Ollie went around and examined the hose from all sides. He was trying to find out how it worked: where the water came from. Dad was watching, his eyes sparkling with pride.

"That one's going to be a plumber," he said.

"You said he was going to be a builder the other day," I pointed out.

"He could be either," Mum replied.

I wasn't impressed. And I felt annoyed with Hercules for playing with Ollie. He was meant to be my dog – whatever happened to loyalty? All at once, I could see myself becoming lonelier and lonelier.

Jane must have noticed my expression.

"Don't let it get to you," she said.

"I'm not," I replied. "I just didn't know there was anything so great about hosepipes."

"Your parents like to see Ollie looking happy."

In some ways I could understand that.

After a while, I went back up to my room. There were important things to get on with. I got out my sketchbook and sat by the window, looking out at the road where I had seen Ollie arrive. I drew a picture of my natural mum arriving: she was rushing over to hug me. She was beautiful, tall and she was coming to take me away from Little Meadows.

I didn't quite finish the picture. It didn't seem likely that my natural mum would really show up. I was just trying to make myself feel better and not think about how she didn't want me. I carefully put the drawing under my bed. The last thing I wanted was for Mum or Dad to see it. Maybe I was betraying them a bit with these thoughts about my natural mum – but then they were betraying me by adopting Ollie.

I didn't leave my room until later that night,

when everyone else had gone to bed. It was my usual time for wandering around the house, as I didn't have to worry about bumping into anyone. The plan was to watch some TV in the living-room. On the way past Ollie's room I remembered what Mum had said about me when I first arrived: how I hadn't liked being by myself. I decided to check on Ollie quickly.

He was wide awake, sitting up in his cot and staring out with his big blue eyes. He looked very sad, but he wasn't crying. It was strange: I'd have thought that a two-year-old who couldn't sleep would be making loads of noise. But he was silent.

It would have been mean to just leave him like that and go downstairs so I went over to his cot.

"Everything's OK," I told him.

He looked at me as if he was trying to work out if he could trust me. I tucked him in under his blanket with his cloth next to him.

"You don't need to be sad," I said. "Look, you have your cloth here."

He closed his eyes and seemed to relax. I sat by the window and looked out at the starry night.

I waited until he was asleep and then I crept back to my room, not sure what to make of it all.

CHAPTER TEN

Grandma Kettle let herself in through the front door.

"Ollie!" she called.

Mum brought Ollie downstairs to say hello.

"My grandson," Grandma Kettle said.

She tried to give him a hug, wrapping her bony arms around his shoulders, but he didn't reciprocate – he just froze up and looked tense. I could tell that Grandma Kettle noticed because a puzzled expression flickered across her face. But she carried on all the same.

"You just wait until you see what I've got for you," she said to him.

She led the way into the living-room and started emptying her handbag. All the usual rubble came out in a cloud of dust: old receipts, loose mints, spare knitting needles and lots of coins.

"It's in here somewhere," Gran said.

After a lot of rummaging, she pulled out a blue woollen hat. The name OLLIE was sewn on it in enormous black letters.

"Doesn't this look wonderful?" she said modestly.

"It's beautiful," Mum replied, smiling.

"Do you remember the hat I knitted for you when you first arrived, Chloe?" she asked me.

I nodded.

There was no way I could forget that bright-pink monstrosity with a picture of a kettle on the front. It was one of those things that would always haunt me. Whenever Gran came round, I used to be forced to wear it.

"Well, now Ollie has one of his own," she said, putting it on Ollie's head. "I think it suits him."

"You did a great job," Dad said.

"Talking of great," Grandma Kettle said, scanning the room with a meaningful look in her eye, "why doesn't someone bring Great-uncle Herbert downstairs? Ollie ought to meet all the relatives."

I liked the way she said it: as if the portrait was actually a living person.

"He's hanging on the wall up the stairs," I said.

"I know and I'm not pleased, not pleased at all. He was meant to be a centrepiece for the living-room, not hidden away in the shadows where no one can see him," Grandma Kettle replied.

As far as I was concerned, the shadows were the best place for him. The more shadows to hide that creepy face, the better. But no one was asking my opinion.

"Chloe, you wouldn't mind getting him, would you?" she said.

It wasn't a question: it was an order. I thought my parents could have at least stuck up for me. But Mum just made it worse.

"Ollie could help you, Chloe," she suggested.

"I don't want to carry the picture *and* Ollie around the place."

But Ollie seemed quite enthusiastic to get away from the adults, so I let him come with me.

I carried him upstairs.

"Why am I always the one who gets bossed around?" I complained. "By the time you grow up, no one will bother you because they'll be worn out from ordering me about."

He looked up at me, not understanding. His hat was too big for him; it had slipped down over his forehead.

At the top of the stairs, I unhooked the portrait.

"Isn't it ugly!" I whispered. "Grandma Kettle can't really expect us to hang it in the living-room. I won't be able to go downstairs and watch TV at night with that thing staring at me."

Ollie seemed to agree with me. He didn't say anything, but he pointed at the picture and made a face.

"You don't speak much, do you?" I said. "I thought you'd cry and be in the way all the time, but you're actually quite quiet. Now, shall we go find out what's happening in the living-room? I bet Gran is going to talk about Great-uncle Herbert for ages."

I dragged the portrait into the living-room and propped it up next to Gran.

"Thank you, Chloe," she said and then she turned to Ollie. "Why don't you come over here and say hello. Herbert always loved children and he would have especially liked you."

I thought now might be a good time to leave.

"I'm going upstairs," I said.

"Already?" Mum asked.

"I have things to do. I can't stick around here all day."

"Did I tell you about the yellow roses I'm planning to grow in the garden?" Dad asked.

"Yes," I replied.

"You could tell Gran about them," Mum suggested.

"About what, dear?" Gran asked.

"I'm going to grow some yellow roses along by the fence," Dad told her.

"Oh," she replied. "And when are you planning to get a proper job?"

"I'm starting work with the newspaper in town next week."

"He's also writing another book," Mum said.

"Fiction is for people who have nothing better to do with their time..." Gran began.

I edged out through the living-room door. On my way, I glanced over at Ollie. Dad was lifting

him on to the sofa. Ollie seemed really frightened
– much worse than when Gran had hugged him
earlier. He had tensed up as if he expected Dad to
hurt him, which was crazy because Dad was the
gentlest person around.

CHAPTER ELEVEN

Later that evening, I went into the bathroom. Mum was in the middle of giving Ollie a bath. I was just planning to get my comb and some hair gel and leave straight away, but then I saw something that gave me a shock. Ollie's back was covered in all these marks – scars and old burns.

"What happened to Ollie?" I asked.

Mum looked over at me.

"What do you mean?"

"The marks," I said.

"They're from before," she replied.

Mum had told me that Ollie had been abused by his natural dad, but it hadn't really sunk in. Ollie was pushing a yellow rubber duck around the bath. Mum wiped his shoulders with a sponge.

I couldn't move. I could only watch. I wanted to act indifferent about it and like I didn't really care, but I couldn't believe that someone had done this to Ollie.

Then I thought of something else. If this had happened to Ollie "before", then what had happened to me? Had I been beaten up when I was a baby too? There were all kinds of things that could have gone on without me remembering. No one had said I'd been hit, but that didn't mean anything. Mum and Dad could have been saving that bit of information about my past until I was older.

I finally stopped staring and hurried back to my room. I needed to find out the answer to this one. I checked my body for any unusual scars. I looked at my legs, trying to examine every inch. I pulled off my top and went over to the mirror, twisting round to get a view of my back. There were still large areas I couldn't see properly. That was probably where all the scars were.

I dug around my room to find another mirror – I needed to know for sure if there were any marks. I eventually found one in my cupboard.

Using the two mirrors, I could see all of my back. There was a little mole that I hadn't seen before, but that was it. No marks; no scars. I sat down on my bed, relieved. What had I been thinking? Of course no one had beaten me up. My natural mum would never have done something like that. She cared about me and she would have made sure that I was safe.

I got out the drawing of me and my mum that I'd started the day before. There she was, hugging me. That was proof of how important I was to her. I used my coloured pencils to add some more details. I put her in a glamorous designer dress, while I wore jeans with designer holes in them. She was wearing pearls and lipstick. I was smiling in a very exaggerated way, to show how happy I was.

But I couldn't have been that happy. Not in real life. Suddenly I realized that tears were streaming down my cheeks. I wiped them away with the back of my hand. It wasn't as if Ollie and I were close, so why was I so upset about seeing his scars? And why had I let myself think that maybe it had happened to me too?

I would have liked to talk to Mum or Dad about all this, but I didn't feel I could. It wasn't because I didn't think they would listen; it was because they were my parents. They wouldn't understand and it'd be awkward trying to talk to them. So I decided to go over to Kate's house. I tried to make myself look like I hadn't been crying. Then I left my room.

"Mum, I'm going to Kate's," I called through the bathroom door.

"That's fine," she replied. "Just don't be home too late."

I moved away from the door.

Then Mum called after me, "Chloe, you are OK, aren't you?"

There was concern in her voice.

"Yes," I said and dashed downstairs.

CHAPTER TWELVE

I knocked on the door at Kate's house.

"Come in!" a voice called.

Kate was in the kitchen with Angie.

"Hi," Kate said. She must have seen that I was upset because she asked, "What's going on?"

I wasn't sure how to start talking about what I'd seen earlier. But I felt safe talking to Kate and Angie so I just came straight out with it.

"Ollie's got all these burn marks and scars on his back. I saw them while Mum was giving him a bath. It was awful. And then I got really worried that someone might have hurt me when I was little too."

Kate came over and put an arm round me.

"I looked in the mirror and couldn't find any

marks," I continued. "I suppose I just got frightened."

"How come Ollie has those scars?" Kate asked.

"I think they're from his natural dad. Mum told me that sometimes he hit Ollie so badly that he ended up in hospital," I said.

"It's horrible, the things that go on," Angie said. "It's hard to believe that someone would do that to anyone, let alone such a small defenceless child. Ollie is lucky to have you and your parents looking after him."

"I didn't exactly volunteer myself for the position," I replied.

"Sometimes you have to rise to the occasion."

I wasn't one hundred per cent convinced about that.

I thought I should go back home. I wasn't sure what I expected to find, but I felt like I should check on Ollie. What if he couldn't get to sleep again without me there? I agreed to meet up with Kate again in the morning. She was going to show me around the village.

As I went in through the front door, Hercules started barking in the kitchen. Most of the downstairs lights were off. It wasn't even nine o'clock, but it looked as though my parents had already gone to bed. I made my way quietly upstairs.

"Chloe?" Mum called from her room.

"I'm back," I said. "Good night."

"Night."

Dad was in Ollie's room. I could hear him reading Ollie a story. He put on voices for all the characters. He used to make me laugh loads when he read me stories, but Ollie wasn't laughing. He stayed silent, even at all the funny parts.

I went into my room and waited until Dad had gone to bed. Then I crept into Ollie's room. He was wide awake, staring out from his cot like the night before.

"You don't need to be scared of Dad," I whispered. "He's not going to hurt you."

I brought down a few of Ollie's teddies that had been put up on the shelf.

"They're all coming to say good night to you," I said. "Here's big bear, little bear and the one-eyed cat. They all say, 'good night, Ollie' and they do a goodnight dance."

I made the bears twirl around and then the

one-eyed cat waved.

"See, you're safe here," I told him.

Ollie yawned and lay down, snuggling up to his cloth.

I tiptoed out of the room and headed downstairs.

I got Hercules from the kitchen and we watched TV for a while. The portrait of Great-uncle Herbert was leaning against the wall by the bookshelf. I could feel his eyes watching me and it made me uncomfortable, so I got off the sofa and turned the portrait round.

"That's better," I said.

Then I went back to watching the old black and white film that was on. I wasn't really concentrating very well though: I was thinking about Ollie. Why did I take it as my responsibility to make sure he could sleep? I wasn't the one who'd wanted him to move in. But he was a little boy who needed my help. I couldn't just leave him in his room to be miserable.

Hercules jumped up on to the sofa next to me. He gave me a sheepish look, not sure if he was going to be told off or not. Mum and Dad never let him lie on the sofa, but I wasn't so fussy. If he wanted to be up here, why not let him? It was nicer than the floor. I stroked his ears and he looked content.

"What am I going to do about this new brother?" I said.

Hercules' only answer was to chew my feet.

CHAPTER THIRTEEN

Mum wanted me to watch Ollie for a while the next day. She had a meeting (it had something to do with raising money for the school library – that was all I knew). Dad had started his new job in town. So it was down to me to look after Ollie. Of course, I tried various arguments. I complained about being an unpaid babysitter and said that parents shouldn't take advantage of their children; I also reminded her that it was my summer holidays. But, in the end, it didn't make any difference.

I sat in the kitchen with Ollie. I looked at my reflection on the microwave door and practised making faces. I did my exaggerated happy face, followed by my worst scowl. Then I noticed that

Ollie was copying me.

"Don't copy," I said. "I know you'd rather be out playing with the hose and I'd prefer to be in my room. But we're stuck in this babysitting thing together."

I checked my watch, trying to work out exactly how many minutes were left until Mum came back and I could go.

"It should only be another forty-two minutes and fifteen seconds," I told Ollie.

I showed him my watch.

"You see, this is how we measure the time that passes in a day."

Suddenly I felt like a bit of an authority on the things that went on (and I suppose I was, to Ollie – he listened eagerly to whatever I said). I pointed to the clock on the wall.

"See, that measures time too – like my watch. When you grow up, watches are really important. They tell you how much time you have to wait around."

Hercules came in from the garden. He lay down in his basket, resting his nose on his muddy paws. He had probably been doing more digging.

Dad said that Hercules was trying to change the garden into a mudbath; it was threatening his dream of growing roses along the fence: Hercules might end up eating them for dinner, thorns and all.

"Why don't you draw a picture or something?" I said to Ollie.

It was more interesting than counting down the minutes.

"You could do one of Hercules."

I went over to the drawer and got out a piece of paper and a felt-tip pen. I put them on the table in front of Ollie and pointed at Hercules.

"Hercules likes to have lots of pictures drawn of him. I've got a whole stack of ones I've done upstairs."

Ollie picked up the felt tip and, without taking the lid off, started pressing down on the paper.

"You're not going to get much of a picture like that," I said and took the lid off for him.

This time, he drew lots of big scribbles.

"Don't forget to add a tail and some ears," I suggested (that was if he wanted to make his abstract more dog-like).

I had to hide Ollie's picture when Mum walked in. I hadn't realized so much time had passed. Her meeting was already over.

"What have you two been doing?" she asked.

"Nothing," I replied.

I didn't want to tell her about Ollie doing a drawing. She could get the wrong idea and think that we were getting on. Or else she'd make me babysit even more. I had to try and make it clear that I wasn't happy about all of this.

"You were ages," I said.

"We had a lot to organize."

Mum went over to Ollie and picked him up. She carried him over to the sink and filled a beaker up with orange squash.

"Are my babysitting duties over now?" I asked.

"Yes. Thanks for your help."

"I'm going to meet up with Kate," I said.

"OK," Mum replied. "Just don't make any plans for tomorrow. Jane's coming over to check on Ollie's progress."

"Why do I have to be here? She's not coming to check on me too, is she?"

"Oh, Chloe. Why do you always have to argue?"

"You're the one arguing."

I carefully folded Ollie's drawing under the table and put it in my pocket, so it was definitely out of the way. Then I got up and walked out the front door. Mum was always trying to fill up my time: today it was babysitting; tomorrow the social worker would be here. What had happened to just leaving me alone? I needed time to think and do my own stuff. I might as well not have been on holiday at all. I never got to choose what I did.

Kate was sitting on the bench next to the village pond where we'd arranged to meet. She was throwing crumbs from her pocket for the ducks to eat.

"There you are," she said.

"Sorry I couldn't meet up earlier: I got stuck looking after Ollie."

"Was it that bad?" she asked.

"Not really. But Mum was getting on my nerves. She always orders me around and makes me do things. It's like she doesn't want me to have a life of my own."

"You seemed really upset last night," Kate said.

"Yeah, well ... I can't believe someone would

hurt Ollie like that," I replied.

"It's pretty sick. But at least he's away from his natural father now," Kate said.

"He's not really like a normal two-year-old. He doesn't cry much. I often go into his room at night and find him wide awake."

"He has to get used to being around you lot," Kate said, smiling.

"My family do take a bit of getting used to, I admit. You should see the hat Gran's made for him. But at least she's trying."

We walked around the village. I had already been to most of the places Kate showed me: the playground, the church, the bus stop. But then we went up a country lane and into these woods. The trees were enormous, with maroon and green leaves.

"Further up here, there's this really cool place," Kate said.

"What is it?" I asked.

"My den. I'll take you there sometime, but we need to go on bikes. It's quite a long way away, in an abandoned building. I have posters up there and supplies of coke and crisps and everything."

I liked the sound of that.

"I usually go there when I want to get away from everyone else," she said. "We could go tomorrow if you like."

"I wish I could, but I have to do boring family stuff."

I meant it when I said boring family stuff. I was dreading being stuck with Mum, Ollie and the social worker. I bet Jane would ask me lots of questions; then Mum would get cross when I didn't answer them properly. They would want me to play with Ollie and make something with the building blocks.

When I got home that evening, I tried to get out of it.

"Don't be so negative," Mum said.

"I'm being realistic," I replied.

"Being realistic doesn't mean giving up on everything."

"You want me to be happy and smile all the time."

"Not if you don't feel like it," she said.

"I don't feel like spending tomorrow with Ollie's social worker. Especially when I've made plans with Kate."

I was making up this last part to annoy Mum.

"I told you not to," she said.

"I made these plans last week," I replied. "Way before you said anything about Jane coming here. And I'm not going to change them."

CHAPTER FOURTEEN

The next morning, we were sitting in the living-room with Jane. Somehow I had been persuaded to stick around. I wasn't too pleased about having to get up so early. It was ten-thirty and I felt exhausted. I had tried suggesting to Mum that she should invite Jane to come later on, then I wouldn't have to mess up my sleeping patterns. But of course Mum hadn't listened.

Ollie was sitting next to me on the sofa. His hair had been combed and he didn't have a spot of dirt on any of his clothes (though that wouldn't last long). Mum had even washed his cloth; it actually looked white for once. I hadn't been allowed to wear any of my "scruffy outfits", as Mum liked to call them. She'd tried to get me to wear this gross pink dotty skirt, but I'd told her there was no way I was going around looking like a Barbie doll.

Jane and Mum were chatting away, while Ollie and I sat there silently. I couldn't bring myself to listen to their conversation. Ollie was looking at the table lamp; he seemed curious about how it worked. I tried to think what the world must be like for him, with everything being new and amazing. I took most things for granted, probably because I had seen them so many times before; it stopped me noticing them. But Ollie's fascination still wasn't going to get me too interested in examining a light bulb.

"Watch out," I whispered to Ollie. "You don't want them to go on about how you're going to become an electrician when you're older."

He pulled at my arm, trying to get me to go over and look with him.

"We're better off staying here," I said. "Anyway, there's nothing that great about light bulbs: they give out light and that's about it. We could make shapes out of your cloth instead."

I made sure Mum and Jane weren't paying attention. Then I reached over to Ollie's cloth and tried to make it look like a bird.

"Look, a white dove," I whispered.

He quite liked that.

"What else can we make? A mountain with snow on top."

I stopped quickly when I noticed Jane looking over. She had a slight smile. I sat back on the sofa and crossed my arms. It wasn't difficult for me to put on one of my scowls (I had a collection, all tried and tested on my parents for perfection).

"Chloe, why are you pulling that face?" Mum asked.

"I'm bored," I said.

"We'd better do something more exciting then," Jane replied. "We could play with the building blocks."

I would have preferred to stay bored.

"Come on, Chloe," Mum said.

She was always harassing me.

"I don't mind sitting on the sofa," I said. "You can all play with the blocks, while I stay here."

"I think Ollie would like it if you joined in," Jane replied.

It wasn't worth the argument. I got up from the

sofa and went over to the blocks that Jane had spread out on the floor. I checked my watch. I would join in for ten minutes then go back to my room and catch up on some sleep: that was the deal I made with myself.

Ollie didn't seem quite sure what to do with the blocks. He tried chewing one of them.

"You don't want to be like Hercules," I told him, "chewing everything."

I pulled it out of his mouth.

"What shall we make?" Jane asked.

I wasn't about to shout out any suggestions.

"How about a castle?" Mum said.

Really, it should have been Jane and Mum left in the living-room to play with the blocks. Ollie and I could have gone off and done something more fun.

"Can you say tow–er?" Jane asked Ollie.

He looked blankly at her.

"Give it a go," she said. "Tow–er."

Ollie still didn't say anything.

"He's very behind at learning how to speak," Jane said to Mum.

"We've been reading to him every night and

trying to encourage him," Mum replied.

I felt a bit stupid. I was probably the last person to realize Ollie had problems learning to speak. I tried to think whether there was anything I could do.

I did have all those signs in my room – the ones I put up on my door. They would be a good place to start. They were nice and big: I could use them to help Ollie speak. I kept this genius plan to myself: I wasn't sure that Jane and Mum would fully appreciate it.

I waited until the castle had been built out of blocks, then I went up to my room (I had stayed downstairs for a whole twelve minutes – two minutes longer than planned).

I reached under my bed for my artistic treasures and pulled them out. I'd have Ollie speaking in no time using these things. The words were in bright colours and some even had little drawings. The "EXPLOSIONS!" sign was made with red letters and the word looked like it had been blown up. The "Go Away!" sign was in blue, with arrows pointing off to the side.

I waited until Mum brought Ollie upstairs for

his afternoon nap. When she'd left, I tiptoed into Ollie's room with the signs tucked under my arm. I found him lying in his cot. He wasn't completely asleep. I only had to nudge his arm a few times and he opened his eyes.

"Hi," I said and showed him the signs. "You're going to learn how to speak. One day, you'll be as good as anyone else at it. But we're going to start with this."

I pointed at the first sign.

"Go aw–ay," I said slowly.

I wasn't really thinking about what the words meant. These were just the words I happened to have on the signs already. And, taken separately, there was nothing wrong with the words "go" and "away" – they were very useful, in fact.

Ollie rubbed his eyes but kept quiet.

"You're going to have to try harder," I said, and repeated, "Go aw–ay."

I had to say it about five more times before I got a response.

"Tha–thay," he said.

"There's no 'th' sound: it's 'g'."

"G," he echoed.

"Brilliant," I said.

I didn't see Mum standing behind me with her hands on her hips.

"Ga–tha–thay," Ollie said.

I hadn't been expecting him to say the whole phrase. I almost gave him a hug, I was so pleased.

Then I heard Mum's voice, "Chloe Adelaide Tulip, what on earth is going on?"

CHAPTER FIFTEEN

Mum was cross with me for teaching Ollie rude words. It didn't occur to her that I was trying to help him learn to speak. Mum and I would never understand each other. I wasn't about to explain anything either. If she wanted to assume the worst, she could.

I was really annoyed with her for calling me by my full name too. She knew I hated it when she did that. She was annoying me on purpose. My natural mum would never have acted that way; she would have appreciated me more. I wished she would come for me.

I got out the drawing I had done of us together and hugged it. If only she would come for me, I wouldn't have to put up with my family for much longer. I would leave them all behind, except maybe Hercules and Ollie. We'd drive out to this enormous house with an artist's studio all for me. I wouldn't have adults annoying me all the time. My natural mum would be grown-up, but she would be different – more like Angie. She'd listen to me and I'd be able to speak to her. I wouldn't have to be so lonely.

She'd read me beautiful stories that she'd written. Most of them would probably be about how much she had missed me. She'd have shelves full of books that she'd had published, letting the world know how she felt. Of course, I would be the heroine of every story. I thought I'd make quite a good heroine really. I just needed some interesting things to happen, instead of being stuck at home with my family. If only I had some dragons and witches in my life, it would make all the difference.

I watched the cars passing by on the road. There was a red one with a woman driving. I wondered for a moment if she was going to stop in front of the house. She could be my natural mum, come to get me at last. I didn't mind that she wasn't driving a limo. Even a clapped-out old car would do. As long as I knew it was her. The red car passed by. It didn't even slow down. So I gave up on car-watching and looked out for pedestrians instead.

I liked being able to imagine a new life for myself. There seemed to be so many possibilities that way. I knew Mum had said my natural mum was a drug addict, but she could have recovered by now.

I only saw one woman walking by. She was holding hands with someone and laughing. I didn't think she looked much like my natural mum (not from my imagination, anyway).

I sighed and closed my eyes. Oh well, it didn't seem like she was coming today. Another day maybe. I would just have to get on with my own life until then. I started doodling in my sketchbook: a pattern in red and blue, with flowers and different shapes.

Then Dad knocked on my door.

"Chloe," he called.

"What do you want?" I muttered.

"I heard about you reading signs to Ollie.

I thought it was nice of you."

So I was being appreciated for once?

"OK, you can come in," I said.

Dad opened the door. He must have just got back from work. He was dressed in a suit, along with an orange and brown checked flat cap (that didn't go especially well with the suit). He perched on the corner of my desk. I thought I'd tell him what happened.

"Jane told Mum that Ollie was having problems learning to speak. I was trying to help, but Mum had to go and freak out."

"You surprised her, that's all. She's not cross any more."

But I was.

"I'm not talking to her today," I said.

"She'll be upset about that."

Dad got up and went to the door. Before he closed it, he looked in one last time.

"I'm making chicken in breadcrumbs for dinner," he said.

"With tomato ketchup?" I asked.

He knew it was my favourite.

"Lots of ketchup."

That was one way to tempt me out of my room.

About twenty minutes later, Dad called, "Dinner's ready!"

I went down to the kitchen. I tried to ignore Mum and focused on the floor instead. Hercules was under the table, hoping someone would drop some food. Ever since Ollie had been around, he'd been doing pretty well.

I sat on my usual chair, closest to the door. Dad put a plate down in front of me. I tried to get the ketchup without looking at anyone. I thought I was doing quite well at ignoring Mum – but then she started talking to me.

"I'm sorry for telling you off earlier," she said.

I started eating with extra speed.

"I didn't know you were trying to help Ollie," she continued. "You could have waited until he'd finished his nap. And there are all kinds of useful books – without rude words."

"I'm not going to bother any more," I muttered, and carried on eating quickly.

It only took me about five minutes to eat my dinner – then I'd been planning to disappear up to my room. But I had to sit and wait for everyone else to finish before I could leave.

"There's no rush," Mum said.

"Stay here and enjoy the company," Dad said, smiling.

I wasn't sure if he was trying to be funny or not.

Hercules was having a much better time than me: Ollie was feeding him pieces of chicken. Mum and Dad were slow to realize because they were busy talking. It was only when Ollie started throwing food that Mum and Dad reacted.

"You two!" Dad said and he took Hercules outside.

Mum cleaned up the mess around Ollie's highchair. Just then, the phone started ringing.

"Can you get that, please?" Mum asked me.

I didn't usually like answering the phone. But I thought there was a small chance it could be Kate and we could arrange to go on a bike ride up to the den. I picked up the receiver.

"Hello?"

"Chloe," Grandma Kettle said, "I need you to come over here right away. It's an emergency!"

CHAPTER SIXTEEN

Gran had these "emergencies" quite often. It usually meant she had lost something. I quickly regretted picking up the phone. I only just managed to get out of going to her house that night (I told her I had to do the washing-up – it sounded like a good excuse). She told me to come over first thing the next day. I agreed, vaguely thinking I'd stop by sometime in the afternoon.

Early the next morning, the phone started ringing again.

"Chloe! Gran wants to know why you're being so slow," Mum called.

I thought I was having a nightmare at first. I turned over on my side and tried to block out the noise. But then Mum came into my room with the phone. She put it on the pillow, next to my ear.

"Where are you?" Gran was saying, obviously in the middle of one of her monologues. "You promised to be here first thing in the morning. I NEED HELP FINDING MY HEARING AID. You don't want me to be deaf all day, do you?"

I climbed out of bed. It was another early start. There must be some sort of conspiracy going on to stop me getting a decent night's sleep. I got dressed and went over to Gran's house. I spent a moment admiring the sign I'd made her. I wondered if I should start charging for them, then I'd have more money to spend.

It would be good to get my sign-making company going. I could just picture it: I would have shops all over the country, where people would go to get their own personal signs made. I could specialize in signs for moody teenagers and walking-stick-wielding grandmas.

I knocked on the door and waited. Suddenly, the bronze letter slot opened.

"Is that you?" Gran asked.

"I think so," I replied.

Gran unlocked the door and let me in.

"You took your time," she said.

"I don't usually get up this early."

"Well, come along. We've got to find that hearing aid. Now, I'm sure it's around here somewhere. It might have fallen behind the sofa."

I took all the cushions off the sofa and couldn't see any sign of it. I crawled around on the carpet, looking behind the TV and pulling back the curtains. Gran disappeared into the kitchen and came back with a pot of tea, along with two cups and saucers. She put them down on the table.

I quickly worked out why Gran had wanted me to come over. It wasn't the hearing aid at all: she was looking for someone to have tea with.

"You'll probably want a break now, dear," she said.

She poured out the tea and handed me a cup. I looked down at the black mixture. I didn't dare take a sip because it looked so strong. I poured in all the sugar and milk that I could. Then I spent a lot of time stirring it around.

"So, how are things at home?" Gran asked.

"Not too bad."

"You must be getting along well with Ollie."

"We get along OK," I replied.

"Ollie's a wonderful little boy. You're so lucky to have him. Brothers and sisters are very precious. One day you'll realize that."

I didn't really fancy getting sentimental. I was about to go back to looking for the hearing aid (even if it wasn't really lost) when she started talking about her brother. I had never really heard her talk about him before; usually it was just the portrait she went on about.

"I had a brother who I was very fond of," she said.

"You mean Great-uncle Herbert?"

She nodded.

"He was a great man indeed. It was a shame though: he fought in the Second World War and never made it back. That just about broke my heart."

"I'm sorry," I said.

I guessed that was why the portrait meant so much to her: it reminded her of him. I glanced over at her fireplace and the bare space above it.

"The portrait would look good there," I suggested.

"I couldn't possibly take it back from your parents," she replied. "They would miss it too much."

I knew that wasn't true.

I didn't stay for much longer. Gran walked me to the door and did her royal wave as I walked away. As soon as I got home, I went up to my room. I sat down on my bean bag and thought about doing some drawing. I even considered going out into the garden (since I had already drawn everything in my room at least five times over).

Then I got a visitor of my own. Ollie pushed open my bedroom door. He was dressed in his pyjamas.

I didn't want to get in trouble again, after disturbing his nap the day before.

"Aren't you meant to be having a nap?" I asked.

Ollie just looked at me. He didn't have a clue what I was saying. Then I remembered that I had the drawing of Hercules he'd done a couple of days earlier. I took it from the pocket of my trousers which were hanging over a chair.

"Let's look at this," I said and moved over so he could sit down on the bean bag too.

I unfolded the drawing.

"Not a bad picture of Hercules," I said. "I'll show you some of the ones I've done of him."

I opened up my drawing pad and flicked through the pictures.

"Hercules," I said, and pointed.

"Luc–thes," Ollie echoed.

I couldn't help smiling: he had managed to say a name.

"Do you know who I am?" I asked.

I decided I'd better help him out. "Chloe," I said, pointing to myself.

"Lo–ee," Ollie said.

"You're getting good!"

He really cheered up when he got a compliment. His whole face lit up and all the worry disappeared for a moment.

"And who are you?" I asked. "Can you say 'Ollie'?"

I pointed at me and then at him. "Chloe and Ollie. That's us."

I heard Mum down in the living-room. She was unpacking her books, trying to sort out where to put them all. But she would probably come upstairs to check on Ollie soon. I thought I'd better take him back to his room.

"It's time for someone to have a nap," I said.

I carried him down the hall and put him in his cot.

"No more climbing out."

He snuggled up with his cloth and teddies and quickly fell asleep. I stayed for a minute. Maybe Gran was right. Maybe I was lucky to have Ollie here after all.

CHAPTER SEVENTEEN

At last, I was free to do what I wanted. Kate and I rode our bikes to the place she'd told me about, where she'd made a den. It was miles away from the village (at least, it seemed like miles to me, but speeding along on a bike had never been my thing. I hadn't had much practice, living up in Edinburgh.) We cycled through the woods and I almost got catapulted into the bushes a few times, as the wheels of my bike kept getting stuck in the ruts.

"Careful," Kate said, turning around to look at me.

It was all right for her: she was used to cycling in the woods.

"Don't they have cycle paths around here?" I asked.

"Not in the countryside," Kate replied.

"I really think they should. I could easily get a puncture," I said.

"Do you think there should be shops and news stands along the way too?" Kate asked.

"I know the woods are pretty and everything, but they do go on a bit," I said, looking around at the trees.

"You're not used to them, that's all. You've been spending too much time in your room," Kate replied.

"Or over at Gran's, searching for her things."

"Sounds like she's enough to drive anyone crazy," Kate said.

"But she had a special message for me this time. She said that I was lucky to have Ollie as my brother."

"Did your parents ask her to say something to you?" Kate asked, looking back at me (I was having a hard time keeping up).

"I don't know," I replied.

"I bet they really want you to get along with Ollie," she said.

"We do get along OK, but I could do without Mum and Dad knowing that," I said.

"In case they pat themselves on the back and say that they knew it would end like this?" Kate asked.

"Something like that. It also really got on my nerves yesterday when Mum told me off, and I was only trying to help Ollie learn to speak. I used some of my signs: they were perfect."

"What sort of signs?" asked Kate.

"I hang them on my bedroom door. They say things like 'Leave me alone', 'Knock if you want an argument'," I said.

"No wonder your mum wasn't happy. All she needs is someone else going around saying 'Leave me alone.'"

"You mean a two-year-old who talks like a teenager?" I asked.

"Yes, a double headache," Kate said, with a smile.

"I think it would have been funny," I said.

"Imagine your Gran coming over and Ollie saying rude stuff to her," Kate said.

"She probably wouldn't hear it anyway: her hearing aid would start playing up," I replied.

When we got out of the woods, there was an amazing view. The fields looked like patchwork.

There were horses grazing in the distance and a shining stream. It was so green and golden that it was almost overwhelming.

"Look," Kate said.

She pointed to an old stone building. There were these enormous holes in the roof and birds were nesting in the rafters. The windows and doors were hollow openings, but some walls were still standing and there were rooms inside.

"Welcome to my den," Kate said.

We left our bikes in the long grass and went into the building.

The rooms were dusty, with piles of rubble around the place from where some of the walls had fallen down.

"Is it safe?" I asked.

I was afraid the roof might suddenly collapse on us.

"This building's been standing for years. There's no reason why it should fall down now."

"Maybe because it's old and no one looks after it?" I suggested.

"I do," Kate said.

She had decorated the largest room. There were

posters taped to the walls and some cushions in the corners, also a tie-dyed sheet covering the floor. She had some half-melted candles along one side of the room. I was seriously impressed.

"You could live here," I said.

"I'm keeping it as a back-up place," Kate replied.

"What for?" I asked.

"You know, if social services ever tried to move me to another home, I'd run away and come here," she said.

"But you get along really well with Angie," I said.

"You never know what's going to happen next. That's what I've learned. You think everything is OK, then it's not," she replied.

"How many foster families have you had?" I asked.

Kate counted on her fingers.

"This is my seventh."

"It would be cool if Angie could adopt you," I said.

"It's not that easy. Social services aren't sure if it's the best place for me, because of Angie's ex-husband. He was quite violent," she replied.

"But that's not her fault, is it?" I asked.

"No, but social services say I don't have much of a father figure. It's stupid: I'm just about grown-up now. How much longer do they want me to wait for a family? I don't want to be moved again. I like living with Angie."

"I doubt they'll try to move you," I said.

"I hope you're right."

I sat down on some boxes. Then I noticed they were full of books. There were also books scattered around the place.

"How did you get all of these here?" I asked.

"I used my backpack and brought about five or six at a time," Kate replied.

She sat down on some cushions and picked up a book with a stripy bookmark.

"You could stay up here reading for the rest of your life," I said.

"That lot would last about six months," Kate said, glancing over at the boxes.

"My mum's always trying to get me to read. She puts books on my desk in the hope that I'll read them."

"What do you do? Read the back cover then

return them?" Kate asked.

"If I like the back cover a lot, I might read the first few pages. Then other things come up and I get distracted," I said, shrugging.

"But doesn't your dad write books?" Kate asked.

"Yes, he reads me bits from them sometimes and I like that," I said.

"You're just lazy," she replied.

"There are just other things I prefer doing: like drawing. I drew this picture of me and my natural mum," I said.

"Do you think about her a lot?" Kate asked.

"I sometimes wonder what she's like and, when I'm upset, I tell myself she's going to come and take me away," I said.

"Like in a fairy tale," Kate said.

"Do you ever think about your natural parents?" I asked.

"Yes," she replied, then she paused. "I still see my mum every couple of months. That's another reason why I can't be adopted: Mum and I want to stay in touch."

I thought it was amazing: she actually knew her natural mum.

"What's she like?" I asked.

"She has schizophrenia. She's fine sometimes. But she can also get very confused, thinking there are people following her, and hearing voices that say mean things. I lived with her until I was eight," Kate said.

"That must have been difficult," I replied.

"I used to feel like I was the one looking after her. Even though I was little, I knew there was something wrong. But she wouldn't go to the doctor," Kate said.

I stood up and went over to the window. I gazed out at the fields that stretched into the distance.

"Do you ever miss your mum?" I asked.

"All the time," Kate replied. "Though it's not always so great when I do see her. She makes me feel bad about myself. She doesn't mean to. But she'll start going on about how I'm too skinny and don't wear enough clothes."

"She must love you though," I said.

"Yes, but that doesn't always make things easier," Kate replied.

I started thinking about what Mum had told me about my natural mum. I'd wanted to tell Kate about it for ages, but I'd been too embarrassed.

"Apparently my natural mum was a drug addict," I said. "One day, she left me in her flat and didn't come back for two days."

"She probably didn't know how to look after herself – let alone you," Kate replied.

"But she might be better by now," I said.

I couldn't let go of this hope.

CHAPTER EIGHTEEN

The next day, I went out into the garden. I thought I'd start by doing a sketch of the apple tree. One of things I liked about drawing was that it meant I didn't have to think or worry about anything. I could just get on with the picture. It was peaceful somehow.

Mum came outside. I was listening to my Discman, so I couldn't hear her.

"How many times do I have to ask you?" she said.

I took my headphones off.

"Can you watch Ollie for a bit, please? Angie's coming over to help do some cooking for the bake-sale in town."

"Mum, I'm in the middle of something."

"I know, but he won't be much bother."

About ten minutes later, Ollie and I were sitting on the grass together.

"I don't know why I always have to babysit," I said. "You could have helped them with the cooking; I bet you'd be really good at it."

Hercules came running over. He got hold of some of my drawing pencils and started chewing them.

"That's not food, Hercules," I told him crossly.

I tried to pull what was left of the pencils out of his mouth. He rolled over on to his back, hoping I would rub his tummy.

"I don't think so," I said.

I passed Ollie my sketchbook and a pencil that hadn't been chewed.

"Do you want to have a go at drawing the apple tree? Trees are probably easier to draw than dogs: You can do lots of scribbles and they'll look like branches."

Ollie didn't have any problem doing the scribbles. He drew the tree using a bright blue pencil. I passed him a red one for the apples.

"Make some circles, kind of bunched together."

He didn't quite manage that, but there were plenty of red scribbles. I turned over the page so he could start another picture.

"You could try doing *little* patches of red this time," I said.

I did some to demonstrate, and he copied.

"That looks much better," I said.

He was quite enthusiastic, so I thought we could try drawing leaves next (or at least some patches of green).

I picked up a green pencil and scribbled with it.

"These are the leaves," I said, pointing. "Like those ones up in the trees."

Ollie stared up at the sky, missing the tree altogether. I picked some leaves from a low branch and showed them to him.

"Leaves," I said.

"Eaves," he echoed.

"Good. Now you try drawing them."

I handed him the green pencil. He didn't look at the leaves, but he tried to copy what I had drawn.

Then the back door opened. I quickly snatched away Ollie's picture. The last thing I wanted was for Mum to think we were sitting out there drawing together. Angie walked over to us. She had the usual friendly sparkle in her eyes. She was wearing a long flowery dress and her wavy hair was tied up in a loose bun.

"Hello, Chloe," she said.

"Hi," I replied. "How's the cooking going?"

"Very well. We've made lots of cakes and biscuits." Angie saw my sketchbook. "So, what have you been drawing?" she asked.

Reluctantly, I opened the sketchbook and showed her Ollie's picture. She bent down to get a closer look.

"That looks good," she said.

"I suppose," I replied.

Angie turned to Ollie.

"And how are you?" she asked. "Are you behaving yourself? Not annoying your sister too much?"

Ollie was walking around, picking up chewed-up pieces of pencil and putting them in a pile next to the tree.

"Lo–ee," he said and reached out to me.

"He knows your name," Angie said, smiling. "I think that's the first time I've heard him talk."

"He can say Hercules' name too," I said.

"It must be so exciting to see him learning new things. Anyway, I'd better go inside and help your mum. I told her I would just come out and say hello to you two quickly."

She went back into the kitchen. Hercules tried to follow her, but she shut him out. He wandered over to the hose. Ollie wanted to go over there too. He pulled at my sleeve.

"I don't really like hosepipes," I said.

But Ollie was so persistent that I went in the end.

I turned on the tap and Ollie ran the hose into the drain. Hercules barked and Ollie clapped; they were having a great time.

"We don't want to make too much noise," I said. "Mum might come out. How about we use some buckets to collect up the water?"

I quickly went over to the shed and brought out all the buckets I could find. There was a leaky one with holes, another that had lots of dents and one with a rusty handle.

"We can try filling them up."

I used the hose to fill the leaky bucket. Ollie

thought it was really funny when water started coming out of the holes in the side.

I was about to start filling up the dented bucket, when Mum came outside.

"You two are soaking wet," she said.

I looked down and saw that my trousers and top were drenched. Ollie's clothes were soaked too. We were literally sitting in a big puddle.

"I was just trying to get Ollie away from the hose," I said. "He was making this mess everywhere."

Mum shook her head: she didn't seem to believe me. I wasn't sure why, when I told such good lies.

"You'd better go inside and dry off. Angie and I are going to the bake-sale – to sell some of these cakes."

CHAPTER NINETEEN

I managed to persuade Mum to give me my pocket money before she left.

"You're not supposed to have it until Saturday," she said.

"Please! I'll take Ollie to the shop with me."

"OK then. Just be careful crossing the road. Make sure you hold Ollie's hand."

"Mum, I know how to cross a road. We'll be fine."

She gave me two pounds fifty. I helped to carry the cakes and biscuits out to the car. Then Mum and Angie set off, the back seat piled with goodies. Ollie and I stood by the gate, waving.

"Free at last," I said under my breath.

I didn't really mind babysitting as much as I

pretended to – especially now I had my pocket money.

"We might as well go to the shop then," I said to Ollie. "You can buy some sweets if you like."

I walked along the path, Ollie following close behind me. When we reached the road, I held his hand to cross. As we walked towards the shop, I heard two old women talking.

"It's such a shame about all these teenage mothers."

"I swear they start having them younger and younger."

They went quiet as we walked by. But I got a significant look. I could feel myself going bright red – I was so embarrassed.

I hadn't thought about this before: how people might mistake Ollie for my son. I was very mature-looking for my age (not). And of course I acted very grown up too (although my parents wouldn't be in any rush to agree with that one). But I supposed all teenagers looked the same to old people, just like all old people looked the same to teenagers. They probably couldn't tell if I was thirteen or eighteen.

I was careful not to hold Ollie's hand as we went into the shop. I kept my distance.

"MUM will be home soon," I said, with a bit of extra volume so there would be no more confusion.

A few people looked in our direction.

"Don't let them think I'm your mum," I whispered to Ollie.

I usually spent a lot of time in the shop going through the magazines. There never seemed to be any point in buying them, not if you could stand there and read them. And I didn't have enough money. I had told my parents quite a few times that I should get more pocket money – everyone I knew got more than me.

Ollie set off around the shop, playing parachutes with his cloth. He disappeared over by the frozen food section and I had to run after him. I could tell the shopkeeper wasn't too pleased with all this chaos. She glared at us through heavily made-up eyes, but didn't say anything. I helped Ollie pick out a little bag of sweets and I got some strawberry-flavoured chewing-gum.

"This is my brother," I said to the shopkeeper.

She just nodded, not especially interested. I put

a pound coin on the counter and she gave me some change. Then Ollie and I headed out of the shop. There was no sign of the women who had thought I was a teenage mother.

I didn't feel like going home quite yet.

"Do you want to go to the playground?" I asked Ollie.

He was busy digging into his bag of sweets.

I hoped there wouldn't be too many people at the playground at this time of day. I checked my watch: it was nearly two o'clock. I wasn't sure if it was likely to be quiet or not. We'd have to go and check.

We walked a little way up the hill and turned down the path to the playground.

"We might not actually stay," I told Ollie. "We're only looking."

He didn't seem to understand where we were going, but he was happy enough following me.

"I can't believe those women thought you were my son," I said. "We're not even related really."

I tried to work out if we looked similar. We didn't really: he had light reddish hair and blue eyes. I had dark hair and greenish-brown eyes. He was a bit chubby, while I was very skinny. But maybe we were alike in the way we acted. Especially since Ollie tried to copy me all the time now.

I knew this business of having a little brother wasn't going to be easy. I was having to look at myself in a completely different light, now that I had this new identity of big sister. I was used to being an only child, but now I had someone else to look out for. It was very confusing.

When Ollie and I got to the playground, we found it pretty much empty. There were two boys playing on the slide, but no sign of any mums with little children. I felt safe.

"Shall we go on the swings?" I suggested to Ollie.

I lifted him up on to the one for toddlers, with supporting bars around it. I sat on the normal swing and started to push myself through the air, soaring higher and higher. I imagined I could take off like a bird and fly away.

Then I saw that Ollie's swing wasn't moving. He was just sitting there watching me. I slowed down and tried to push him along with me.

"Imagine you're a bird flying through the air," I said. "You have to move your legs if you're going to get anywhere."

He didn't seem to really get the hang of it. But he did bring out his cloth and wave it around.

"All right. Pretend you're on a boat with a big white sail."

He started laughing as his cloth flapped around in the air.

"We're sailing across the ocean, under the endless blue sky," I said. "There are seagulls flying around us as we get closer to land."

We gradually came to a stop.

"That was fun, wasn't it?" I said.

Ollie looked slightly green, as if he was feeling seasick.

I saw a woman with a pushchair coming towards the swings and decided it was time to go.

It'd been great spending time with Ollie and teaching him new things. He actually paid attention to what I said, and this made me feel important and like I had something to offer.

That evening, Kate phoned.

"Do you want to go out to the den tomorrow?" she asked.

"Yeah, that would be cool," I replied.

"We could take some supplies," she said.

"I'll bring some snacks from the kitchen," I offered.

This was going to be fun. I couldn't wait: we could have a feast in the den. And at least no one could ask me to babysit Ollie two days in a row.

CHAPTER TWENTY

The next morning, I took my backpack down to the kitchen and filled it up with food. I got a block of cheese, some tomato-ketchup-flavoured crisps and a bar of cooking chocolate. Then I collected my bike from the side of the house and rode over to Kate's house. She was waiting for me by the gate. She'd also brought a backpack. It looked even more stuffed than mine.

"What did you bring?" I asked.

"I found a few spare cushions up in the attic. I thought they'd make the den more comfortable. I also brought some biscuits. Angie had a supply of about ten packets in the cupboard. She shouldn't miss one or two."

We set off down the country lane. I was getting

better at cycling and didn't get the wheel stuck in so many ruts this time. It was relaxing to feel the wind blowing on my face.

"Do you still think there should be a cycle path out here?" Kate asked.

"Not now. I'm OK," I replied.

"There would be loads of other people riding bikes along here if they made a proper path. It's much more fun like this," Kate said.

I started thinking about yesterday, when Angie was at my house, baking cakes.

"I hope Angie's not going to be friends with my mum now," I said, feeling worried.

"Why?"

"She might tell Mum everything I said about Ollie."

"No, she wouldn't."

I wasn't one hundred per cent convinced.

"I kind of wish Ollie had come to live with us when I was eight or nine, instead of now," I said. "Then he wouldn't be so much younger than me – there wouldn't be such a big age gap."

"He wasn't around then. No one had even thought about him being born. Really, it's only chance that your parents found him at all," Kate replied.

"It's weird when you think about all the different places you could have ended up," I said. "I didn't choose to live with Mum and Dad either. It was all chance. I might never have known Ollie. Hercules might never have been my dog..."

"And so on," Kate replied.

Once I'd started on the "what if" speculations, I couldn't stop thinking about them.

"What if I'd never moved to Little Meadows? We wouldn't be friends."

"You weren't so happy about moving here before."

"I don't mind now I'm used to it."

Eventually we arrived at the den. We left our bikes lying in the grass and ran down the bank to the old building. I had worked out what I liked so much about this place: it was mysterious and sort of lonely. We could have been in the twelfth century, or back in any time in the past. There were no modern buildings or cars in sight. Though I suppose our den had posters and things.

Kate pulled the cushions out of her backpack.

"This place could do with some more decorating. You could come out here and do your drawings, then stick them on the wall. You wouldn't ever have to worry about people disturbing you," she said.

"I've been wanting to draw more outside," I replied. "I did a sketch of the apple tree in my garden a few days ago. Ollie drew some pictures of it too."

"Have you been showing him how to draw?"

"I've tried to. But mainly he just does lots of scribbles in different colours."

I sat down on one of the cushions and emptied my backpack. The crisps fell out, along with the chocolate and the cheese. Kate added her biscuits to the pile.

"This is a real picnic," she said.

There were no plates or knives, so I had to bite right into the block of cheese.

"We're like mice," Kate said, smiling.

"Hanging out in a field," I replied. "I used to dream about running away and living in the woods – when I was about ten. It wasn't because I was angry with my parents. I just thought it sounded like a fun idea. I'd pack some of my stuff and plenty of food. I'd also bring some friends along. It would be an adventure."

"Let me know when you're going," Kate said.

"We can just come here instead," I replied.

We spent the rest of the afternoon trying to make our den look better. We moved the tie-dyed sheet that was covering the floor and hung it over one of the holes in the wall. Then Kate took the cushions to her end of the room and I set up my area. I tried to make a space where I could come and do my drawings in the future. It was right by the window, with a beautiful view of the hills and valleys.

We cycled home in time for dinner. Angie came out of Kate's house as we pulled up outside. She waved at me.

"Hi, Chloe," she said.

"Hi," I replied.

"You two *have* been for a long bike ride. You must have gone to Oxford and back!"

"No, not that far," I said.

"Well, it's good for you to go out and get some exercise. I'm always telling Kate she shouldn't spend so much time in her room."

"Angie," Kate complained.

"Sorry, I won't say anything else," she said, smiling.

I walked my bike back home. There wasn't far to go, so I didn't bother cycling. I decided that I shouldn't worry about Angie being friends with Mum: she could still be my friend too.

Mum was in the kitchen when I got home.

"Did you have a good time?" she asked.

I nodded.

"I need you to keep tomorrow free because Jane will be here. She thinks Ollie isn't speaking enough and I know he usually says more when you're around," she said.

"It has nothing to do with me," I replied.

"She'll only be here in the morning, then I'm meeting with my reading group after lunch. I'd really appreciate it if you could look after Ollie for a couple of hours."

"So, basically, I have to stay at home all day," I said.

"Only a small part of the day. You can do whatever you want as soon as I get back," Mum replied.

I was really annoyed about Mum filling up another one of my days.

"These are meant to be my holidays," I said. "I have my own things to get on with."

I couldn't believe she just expected me to stick around there with the social worker. But there didn't seem to be any way of getting out of it.

CHAPTER TWENTY-ONE

In the end, I did go down to the living-room when Jane arrived, but I got really bored listening to her and Mum talk about Ollie the whole time.

"He seems more confident, but he still doesn't speak very much," Jane said.

"He says one or two words," Mum replied.

Ollie tried to get me to play with the teddies that Mum had brought down from his room. But I wasn't interested. I left him to play by himself.

The portrait of Great-uncle Herbert wasn't in the room any more. Mum had moved it back to the old place, on the stairs. He'd given me a fright the night before. I'd been on my way downstairs to watch TV with Hercules, when suddenly I'd seen Great-uncle Herbert looking down at me.

I'd tripped, and gone down the stairs much faster than I'd planned.

I had a bruise to prove the trauma I'd been through, but I hadn't got the sympathy I deserved. I told Mum about it, but she said she couldn't even see it and put her glasses on. Then she said it didn't look life threatening and asked why I'd been going downstairs in the middle of the night anyway.

I decided that I didn't want to stick around in the living-room any longer. I checked in my pocket. I still had 50p left from my pocket money, so I thought I might as well go and spend it.

I stood up and announced, "I'm going to the shop."

"Right now?" Mum asked.

She was frowning.

"It's all right," Jane said. "If they want to pop out for ten minutes, I don't mind. It can't be very interesting listening to us talk."

"Will you take Ollie with you?" Mum asked.

I would have done, but, at that moment, I was really annoyed that Mum just assumed I'd babysit whenever she wanted.

"I'm going by myself," I said.

I walked towards the living-room door.

"I'm sure he'd like to go too," Mum said.

Ollie was watching. He stood up, waiting for me to call him. But I didn't.

As I was walking up the road, I kept thinking that I should go back and get Ollie. I had wanted him to come with me really. But then, maybe I was feeling too moody to be around anyone. I was better off just being by myself until I cheered up again.

I went into the shop and flicked through some magazines, trying to pass the time. There was no sign of the old women from the other day. A different lady was working at the till as well. I decided to get a can of Coke.

"Is that all, love?" she asked.

I nodded and handed her my 50p.

Then I went to the playground and sat on a swing. I remembered how much fun I'd had playing with Ollie there. I told myself to stop being so depressed. All I needed to do was think of more good things. I thought of the time Ollie had come into my room when he was meant to be having a nap and had looked at my drawings of Hercules.

He'd also learnt how to say my name: Lo-ee. I couldn't help smiling at that.

Things had been so much better since Ollie arrived. I'd been really angry at first, but then I'd realized he wasn't the one annoying me: it was my parents. They had created all this change in my life. I also resented being told that my natural mum was a drug addict. I couldn't make myself believe it (even if it was true). I wanted my natural mum to carry on being what I imagined her to be: a famous poet or something... Anything but a person who spent her time sticking needles into her arms.

I swung higher and higher on the swing. There was something liberating about the rush of energy I felt. I slowed down so I could jump off without hurting myself. I landed on my feet and stumbled forward. It was time to go: I'd been out for nearly an hour and, chances were, Jane would have left by now.

As I walked back up the road to my house, I noticed a brown battered-looking car parked at the side of the road. It was near my house, but not right in front of it. I got this horrible creepy feeling. I don't know why, but it felt like someone was watching me.

I glanced towards the car, trying to be subtle about it, and saw a man sitting in the front seat. The window had been partly wound down and I could see his face. He turned away quickly when he saw me looking at him but he had definitely been watching me. No question about it. He looked scary. I felt a sudden chill, and hurried home.

CHAPTER TWENTY-TWO

By the time I got home, Jane had left. Mum was annoyed with me for disappearing for such a long time.

"It was rude of you, Chloe," she said. "And you upset Ollie. He was crying."

Now I felt even guiltier than before.

"I just needed some time alone," I replied.

"Well, I hope you're feeling better now. I've got to rush off to meet up with my reading group. You don't mind watching Ollie for an hour, do you?"

Ollie was sitting on the stairs holding his cloth.

"No, that's fine," I replied.

"Thanks," Mum said. "I've put some lunch in the microwave for you."

Then she was gone.

I hadn't had a chance to tell her about the man I'd seen in the car. I might have been overreacting – wasn't that what everyone said I did all the time? It was probably nothing. But it frightened me when I thought about him watching me.

I picked Ollie up and carried him into the kitchen.

"What have you been doing?" I asked. "Did you make more things with the building blocks? I'm sorry I didn't take you to the shop with me."

I put Ollie on a chair.

"Now, let's see what Mum left me in the microwave. I hope it's not something disgusting and healthy."

It was chicken nuggets and chips, fresh from the freezer.

"Yummy," I said.

I started heating it up.

Ollie watched the food going round in the microwave. He seemed fascinated by the way the plate was moving in circles.

"The food is heating up," I said. "Microwaves are very clever: they can do things like that. They're a bit like ovens, only they work faster."

I pointed at the oven.

"You see, that's an oven. They take up much more space. When I'm older and have my own place, I'll just have a microwave."

The microwave made loud beeping noises. I took the plate out and put it on the table. I got an extra plate from the cupboard and cut up a few chicken nuggets for Ollie.

"Here's some for you. I'm not sure if you've already eaten, but I don't want you to miss out if you haven't."

I looked over at his high-chair and wondered if I should put him in it.

"You don't need to sit all the way up there, do you? You're fine sitting next to me."

He could only just see over the top of the table. But he seemed happy enough.

Hercules came rushing in from outside. He must have smelt the food. He eagerly watched us eat, quickly gulping down anything that was dropped. Ollie was doing a good job of flicking food across the room. I wasn't sure if he meant to exactly. He just wasn't very good at using his spoon.

"That's the cool thing about babysitting,"

I said. "No one is here to tell us what to do. We can make all the mess we like."

Then Hercules started barking. I didn't take any notice at first (he barked at anything – even if an ant passed by the door). But he didn't stop. I put the plates in the sink and tried to quieten him down.

"Hercules will deafen us all with that noise," I told Ollie.

"Luc–thes," he echoed.

"Yes. He's one noisy dog."

Hercules ran out of the kitchen and over to the living-room window. I shut him in the room.

"I'll let him out again in a minute," I said to Ollie.

I was just walking back to the kitchen, when there was a knock at the front door. I guessed it must be someone from Mum's reading group coming to the wrong house (that happened quite often). Or else it could be a neighbour coming to complain about all the noise Hercules was making (though he hadn't been barking for that long).

I couldn't make up my mind whether to open the door or not. Chances were it wouldn't be anyone coming to see me. I'd be stuck having to pass on messages to Mum or Dad. I decided to pretend there was no one in.

"Come on," I whispered to Ollie. "Let's go into the kitchen."

Then there was a second knock at the door. This time it was much louder, and sounded more violent. People from the village didn't knock like that. Suddenly, I remembered the man in his car out on the road.

But I didn't have time to do anything, because he came crashing in.

CHAPTER
TWENTY-THREE

The man was obviously really drunk. He couldn't even stand up properly – he was swaying. I didn't know what to do. I wanted to run, but I was too shocked to move. I could hear Hercules barking like crazy in the living-room. He was jumping up against the door and growling. I wished more than anything that I hadn't shut him in.

I looked down at Ollie. He was terrified. I'd never seen anyone look like that before. Every bit of confidence he had got since living with us had drained away.

"Ollie?" I whispered.

For a second, I almost forgot about the man, I was so worried. But I wasn't the only one saying his name.

"Oliver," the man said and lunged towards him.

I knew I couldn't let this happen. I pushed the man as hard as I could, so he stumbled backwards on to the floor. Then I picked Ollie up and sprinted upstairs. I ran into my room and pushed Ollie under the bed, then crawled in after him.

"We've got to be really quiet," I whispered. "We don't want him to hear us."

Ollie didn't look like he was going to make any noise. He was completely silent. He seemed to have withdrawn into himself. It was more like his shell that I was trying to protect; the real Ollie was somewhere else.

"We're going to get out of this," I promised. "I'll look after you."

I heard footsteps coming upstairs. I felt sick. I wanted this to all go away. Why weren't Mum or Dad here? They would have known what to do. But it was only me and Ollie.

There were crashing noises coming from Ollie's room.

"I'll find you!" the man shouted.

I was terrified he'd come in here next. I didn't want to be trapped. We had to get away. I crawled back out from under the bed, taking Ollie with me.

I rushed out into the hall. As we reached the top of the stairs, the man was just leaving Ollie's room. His face looked swollen and full of rage.

"It's time to go home!" he said.

He didn't really seem to have noticed me. He was just looking at Ollie. Then he came charging towards us. I backed up against the wall and knocked into something. The portrait of Great-uncle Herbert came crashing down, landing between us and the man. This gave me and Ollie enough time to get away. Holding on tightly to Ollie, I ran downstairs and out the door.

I ran and ran, only vaguely aware of the sun-light on the rooftops and the weight of Ollie in my arms. I found myself knocking at a door and Angie was there. She was staring at us. Then she was taking us inside. She wanted to lift Ollie from my arms, but I didn't want to let go.

"I'm only going to put him next to you," Angie said. "He's not going anywhere."

I let her take him then because I was feeling really faint.

"What on earth has happened?" Angie asked.

"A man broke into the house ... trying to get Ollie," I gasped.

I had to rest my head in my arms.

I could hear Angie on the phone, but she sounded like she was at a great distance.

"An intruder at number eight, Thatcher's Pike Road. I'm phoning from..."

Kate must have come into the room. She brought me a glass of water.

"Oh, Chloe," she said.

She pulled up another chair, giving me a concerned look.

Suddenly, I got this dreadful fear. Where was Ollie? Had I left him at home somewhere? I was afraid I might have failed him dreadfully. But no, there he was sitting next to me. His cloth was missing, though. He must have dropped it somewhere. But Ollie didn't seem to have noticed. He wasn't crying. In fact, he was very still and silent.

Angie was there now too. She was asking, "Are you hurt?"

I shook my head.

"And Ollie?"

I could see her checking him.

"I don't think so," I said.

"You two have been very brave," Angie said.

I didn't feel very brave. In fact, I had never felt so afraid in my life.

Soon there was a crowd of people around me. Mum and Dad were there, and the police. I was asked some questions and I tried to say what had happened. But they all seemed to know more than me and I wasn't sure if I was even making any sense.

"He came in through the front door. We hid upstairs. He wanted to take Ollie. I ran here."

I thought I knew who the man was, but I didn't want to think that the person who'd hurt Ollie before had just turned up at my house. Next to me, my parents were talking to the police. It was then that I heard the words: Ollie's biological father.

CHAPTER TWENTY-FOUR

That evening, Mum and Dad tried to explain everything to me.

"Ollie's father has a serious drinking problem," Dad explained. "He has these blackouts when he doesn't know what he's doing. It's usually then that he goes looking for Ollie."

We were sitting in the living-room. Ollie was next to me on the sofa. He was as silent as before.

"How did he know where we lived?" I asked.

"The police think that he must have followed Jane when she came here earlier today," Mum said. "There's no other way he could have got our address. Social services were especially careful to make sure he didn't get it."

"You see, it's happened before," Dad continued.

"Not here, but at his last foster home."

"Is that why they didn't adopt him?" I asked.

"Yes. He turned up one day and frightened Ollie's foster mum half to death. She didn't think she'd be able to cope if he came again."

"But we can cope. We're going to keep him," I said.

Mum and Dad didn't answer.

I put my arm around Ollie.

"You're going to get better," I told him, "and you'll stay here and carry on being my brother."

He didn't respond at all.

"Chloe, I know you've had a shock," Mum said. "We can think about those things tomorrow. It will be best if you try and get some rest now."

Sleep was the last thing I felt like. I bet I wasn't going to get any sleep that night. I had about a million thoughts and worries whirling around in my head.

"Is Ollie OK?" I asked.

"He's not hurt physically," Dad said. "You did such a great job looking after him."

"But there's something wrong," I said. "It's like he's all numb inside."

"It must have brought back all the bad memories," Mum replied.

"We told you about him being abused," Dad said.

"Yes, but I looked after him," I said. "I didn't let him get hurt. Now he doesn't even seem to know that I'm here."

I could feel the tears streaming down my cheeks. Mum gave me a hug. She was as upset as I was.

"I'm sure he does know that you're here," she said.

"He'll be better in a day or two," Dad added.

"Ollie needs you now more than ever," Mum said. "He just doesn't know how to show it."

Ollie had this blank look in his eyes. I noticed that he still didn't have his cloth.

"Where's his cloth?" I asked.

"I haven't seen it," Mum said. "Maybe he dropped it somewhere."

"I should go and look for it," I replied.

Hercules came rushing over to me, but he didn't jump up. He could sense that something was wrong.

"We've got to find Ollie's cloth," I said.

For now, that seemed like the only possible cure. If I could find Ollie's cloth, he was more likely to get better and start being himself again. I tried to remember if he'd had it in the kitchen when we were eating chicken nuggets. I looked under the table and checked Hercules' pile of chewed objects that he kept behind his basket. But there was no sign of it.

Next, I went into the hall and searched the floor. Hercules was helping me. He sniffed around by the coat-rack. Then we had a look upstairs. Hercules went to my bedroom door and barked, so I opened it. He disappeared under my bed and came out again with the cloth in his mouth.

"Good boy," I told him.

He wagged his tail and proudly held the cloth. He wasn't so good at letting go of it. I had to open up his mouth and separate it from his teeth.

I ran down to the living-room.

"Look what I've found," I said to Ollie. "It's your cloth!"

He wasn't interested. I waved it in front of him and placed it carefully in his lap.

"Where did you find it?" Mum asked.

"In the place we were hiding earlier," I replied.

I had another go at making Ollie notice his cloth.

"Here goes a boat with white sails," I said, "and now there's a white dove flying past you."

But he just carried on sitting there, staring out blankly.

"I think it's best to leave him alone for now," Dad said. "He needs time to recover."

"I know you're trying to help," Mum added.

I didn't pay attention to them.

"Look, Ollie. Here's a snow-topped mountain."

I put the cloth over my hand, so it balanced on the tips of my fingers.

"Ollie must be tired," Mum said. "How about we take him upstairs?"

Mum carried Ollie up to his cot. She tucked him in and made sure he had lots of his teddies around him.

"You can bring your mattress into our room if you like," Mum said to me. "It might help you sleep better."

"I'll move your things for you," Dad offered.

"No, I'll be all right," I said.

I went into my room and climbed into bed, pulling my duvet around me. I tried not to think about how we had been hiding under the bed earlier. Or about the man trying to find us.

I hadn't realized how tired I was. I soon managed to fall asleep. I had this nightmare that Ollie had gone and I was racing around the house, trying to find him. In each room I went into, there were people I knew: Mum, Dad, Angie, Kate and Gran. But, although I wanted to, I couldn't stop in any of the rooms because I needed to get to Ollie before it was too late. A dark shadowy figure was coming towards me...

I woke up with a start and looked around the room to make sure the figure wasn't there. I sat up and checked the clock: it was three in the morning. I didn't want to stay in my room any longer. But I was too frightened to leave. What if the man was out in the hall? I knew I was being irrational. I tried to tell myself that no one was out there.

I climbed out of bed and left my room, dragging my duvet with me. I went into Ollie's room.

I felt better having someone else nearby. I checked on Ollie. He was asleep, his long eyelashes curled against his cheek. His expression looked troubled. Maybe he was having nightmares too.

I noticed his cloth lying next to the cot. I picked it up and put it next to him. Then I tried to make myself comfortable on the floor. I wrapped my duvet around myself and closed my eyes. I was anxious about what was going to happen tomorrow. Would Ollie be better? I hoped Mum and Dad would let him stay here. I couldn't bear it if they said he couldn't live with us any more.

CHAPTER TWENTY-FIVE

When I woke up, I wasn't sure where I was at first. Then I saw Ollie sitting up in his cot.

"I hope you don't mind me sleeping here. I was having a nightmare about you going missing. So I came to make sure you were all right."

Ollie was still very withdrawn, but he was holding his cloth.

"See, I knew you wanted your cloth really," I told him. "Hercules and I went looking all around the house for it yesterday."

I yawned and tried to work out what time it was.

"You don't have a clock in here."

Mum poked her head around the door.

"Hi," she said. "I brought you some tea and toast."

She came into the room and put the things down next to me.

"Breakfast in bed – almost," I said.

"I came in earlier and saw you there. I didn't want to wake you, but I did bring you a pillow."

"Thanks."

"Jane's downstairs," Mum said. "We've been talking about things. You should come and join us if you feel up to it."

"I think I'm just going to stay here," I replied.

After Mum had left, I got up and went to my room to check the time: it was two-thirty in the afternoon. That was late, even for me. I wondered what they were saying downstairs. It could be important. I crept downstairs and listened at the living-room door.

"After a shock, some children can stay withdrawn for years," Jane was saying. "It might not be anywhere near that long for Ollie, but there's no way of knowing. We'll just have to wait and see."

I hurried back upstairs and went over to Ollie.

"You're going to be OK. I know it."

I sat down by the window and looked out at the fields. Maybe this was all my fault. I should have told Mum about seeing the man in the car. I'd meant to. But Mum had been in a rush to meet up with her reading group. And I hadn't wanted her to think I was overreacting.

Hadn't I wished for my natural mum to come for me? I had been daydreaming about it for ages. I'd even drawn that picture of her hugging me. The limo was going to take us away from Little Meadows. Maybe Ollie's natural dad wouldn't have come if I hadn't wished all those things.

I was definitely a bad person. I thought about how I'd shut Hercules in the living-room to stop him barking. He'd been warning us. He'd have tried to protect us. Instead, it was only by luck that Great-uncle Herbert fell off the wall and distracted the man, giving us enough time to get away. Gran would be pleased: she'd always said what a hero her brother was.

I heard the sound of footsteps coming upstairs. Jane knocked on the door and came in.

"I hope I'm not disturbing you," she said.

"No, I was just thinking," I replied.

It was quite nice to have some more company actually. Especially since Ollie hadn't been making a sound.

"How's Ollie coping?"

"You can see," I said. "He's really quiet. But he likes his cloth again."

"He's lucky to have you here," Jane said.

"Not that I do any good," I replied.

"What do you mean?" Jane asked. "You protected him from his natural dad and you were smart enough to go to Kate's house."

"I was trying to get away and that was where I ended up," I said. "It's all my fault."

Jane sat down by the window seat near me.

"You mustn't blame yourself," she said.

"You don't understand: I saw the man out on the road in his car and I didn't say anything," I replied.

"How were you to know he'd break into your house and try to take your brother?"

"I don't know, but if I had..."

"He was probably waiting for your mum to leave. That's why he was sitting out there in his car."

"I could have stopped all this from happening," I said.

"And you did. You kept Ollie safe and that's what really matters."

CHAPTER TWENTY-SIX

The next morning, I read to Ollie. I wanted to try to get him to respond to something. I just kept on reading and reading. I wasn't sure if it was doing any good. I felt a bit like I was reading aloud to myself, but I carried on until my throat got sore.

Then I got his teddies down from the shelf and put on a sort of puppet show. The one-eyed cat went searching for Ollie.

"Where could he be?" he said.

The yellow canary flew over to him.

"Who are you looking for?" he asked.

"Ollie," said the one-eyed cat. "I've been trying to find him for days and he's nowhere to be seen."

"You could ask the fox," the canary suggested.

I picked up the red fur fox with bald patches

around his ears (where someone must have chewed him).

"Hello, red fox," the one-eyed cat said. "Have you seen Ollie around anywhere?"

The red fox thought about this for a while.

"I have seen him, but I can't remember where."

He looked around the room and then right at Ollie.

"There he is!" the red fox said.

All the teddies gathered along the side of Ollie's cot to have a look.

"That's definitely him," the one-eyed cat said.

Ollie started giggling.

"Did you like that?" I asked.

He made a noise and reached towards the teddies.

I went over to the door and shouted, "Mum! Dad! Come and see!"

They came upstairs. Mum was looking tired. She had been really upset since Jane left.

"What is it?" Dad asked.

"Look, Ollie's smiling!" I said.

"That's brilliant!" he replied and turned to Mum. "I told you he'd be fine."

Mum still wasn't as happy as I thought she'd be. She didn't exactly rush over to Ollie like Dad had done.

Dad lifted Ollie out of his cot.

"Who's my special boy," he said. "Now, let's get you dressed. We could go and look at the hose – your favourite thing."

Dad and I got Ollie dressed. Dad put his T-shirt on the wrong way round and his socks looked like they were inside out, but it was exciting to have Ollie responding to things again. Mum stayed at a distance. She did smile at Ollie, but I could tell something was wrong.

Ollie held on to his cloth as I carried him downstairs. Hercules was barking and jumping around the place. He kept trying to tug away the cloth. So everything was almost back to normal.

We ran the hose into the drain. Then Ollie clapped his hands.

"Wa–ter," I said, pointing.

"Tha–tha," Ollie echoed.

"We could get the buckets out," I told Dad. "He likes filling up the buckets. His favourite is the one with all the holes in the side."

I was going to tell Mum that we'd be careful not to get all wet this time, but she had gone inside.

"What's wrong with Mum?" I asked Dad.

"She's got a lot on her mind," he replied.

But he sounded like he didn't want to tell me any more.

We went over to the shed to get the buckets. Then we had a go at filling them up. Ollie seemed to have cheered up a lot. He also wasn't quite as frightened of Dad. He still didn't like being touched, but at least he didn't tense up as if he expected to be hit.

I heard the phone ring inside the house. Mum must have picked it up, because a few minutes later she opened the bedroom window.

"Gran just phoned," she called. "She says she's coming over to get 'the wounded soldier'."

"Who?" I asked.

"I don't know," Mum replied. "That was all she told me. I thought I'd better warn you."

"She hasn't lost anything?"

Mum shook her head.

"Not this time."

CHAPTER TWENTY-SEVEN

Grandma Kettle walked around the side of the house. She was wearing one of her thick woollen skirts and a cardigan with a brooch on one side, showing a picture of the royal family. She also had her walking stick with her, which she pointed at Dad.

"Playing in the drains," she said. "It will be the sewers next."

"Ollie has been enjoying himself and that's all that matters," Dad replied.

"Yes, I heard what happened. Poor boy. It must have been an awful shock."

Gran went to give Ollie a hug. He tensed up, the same as usual. I tried mouthing to him: don't worry, it's only Gran (since she had her back to me). I also made a funny face to make him smile.

Then Gran came to give me a hug.

"If it ever happens again, you come straight to my house," she said.

"OK," I replied.

"I did have training during the war. I learned how to beat the enemy off my vegetable patch with a garden rake."

"I bet you were good at that," Dad said.

"Of course – I was a natural. The Germans wouldn't have stood a chance with me around. I could have frightened them away from more than one vegetable patch."

Gran led the way inside. When we went into the living-room, I noticed she was looking around a lot.

"So where's the wounded soldier?" she asked. "I've come to collect him."

Dad and I were puzzled.

"I don't know," I said.

For a moment, I thought she had truly gone crazy.

"He must be around somewhere," she continued.

Then it clicked: the portrait!

"Oh, he's upstairs," I said. "I'll go and get him if you like."

"Would you, dear?"

I ran upstairs. I stopped by Mum's door on the way.

"Gran's here!" I called.

"Thanks, Chloe. I'll be down in a minute."

Usually Mum was the first to welcome Gran. I couldn't work out why she was being like this. Ollie was much better. She didn't have anything to be depressed about.

Great-uncle Herbert was leaning against the wall. He had a slight dent in his forehead from when he had fallen off the picture hook. It made him seem stranger than ever because it looked like his face was sinking into the frame. I carried the portrait downstairs and presented it to Gran.

"Here's your wounded soldier," I said.

"Poor Herbert," Gran replied, looking at the dent. "Another war wound."

Then she turned to me.

"He was a hero on the battlefield when he was alive and he's still a hero now he's a portrait."

"He certainly came to the rescue for me and Ollie," I said. "He fell off the wall at just the right time."

Gran was positively beaming now.

"Be sure to thank your great-uncle," she told Ollie. "That scar might be permanent, but I'm sure he would have thought it was for a worthy cause."

Mum came in. Her eyes looked red and a little swollen, as if she had been crying. Gran hobbled over and pulled some tissues from her sleeve.

"Now, what's going on?" she asked. "I want to hear it all."

"Chloe, why don't you take Ollie to get some orange squash?" Dad suggested.

I didn't like being left out. But I decided I'd better go.

"Come on, Ollie," I said.

I carried him out of the room. We didn't go into the kitchen though. We stayed by the living-room door. They must have been talking quietly because I couldn't hear anything for a while, but then Gran shouted, "You can't take my grandson away!"

Mum tried to quieten her down, but she carried on.

"I didn't knit him that hat for nothing. He belongs here," she said.

I went into the kitchen with Ollie. It wasn't very nice for him to hear all this (even if he probably didn't understand it). I certainly couldn't work it out. Why would Mum want to give Ollie away? I knew she cared about him. And he was my brother; he couldn't just go.

I remembered being told how Ollie's natural dad had turned up at his last foster home. That was why the family didn't keep him: they thought it would be too much to cope with. Was Mum going to give up just like them? Was she going to let Ollie be passed on to another family like an unwanted parcel?

"I'll do something," I promised Ollie. "I won't let this happen."

But I just didn't have any idea what I could do.

Ollie could see I was getting upset.

"Lo–ee," he said.

He hugged me and started to cry.

"It's all right," I said.

But he carried on crying. I wasn't sure what to do. Why was everyone so miserable at my house?

I thought everything would change once Ollie was himself again, but things had only changed for the worse.

Mum, Dad and Gran must have heard us. They came into the kitchen.

"What's wrong with Ollie?" Mum asked.

"He probably heard you say that you didn't want him," I replied.

"I didn't say that."

But I started getting really angry. The only things I could say were the words that would hurt the most.

"It was all your fault!" I told Mum. "Ollie's dad would never have come if you hadn't gone out and left us."

"Chloe, that's not fair," Dad said.

"What's not fair is you and Mum planning to send Ollie away without telling me."

"Try to calm down," Gran said. She put her hand on my shoulder. "All this shouting isn't good for my hearing."

I marched out of the house, slamming the front door behind me. I wanted to get away from my parents and never see them again.

CHAPTER TWENTY-EIGHT

I went straight round to Kate's house and told her what had been going on.

"Did they say for sure that they were sending Ollie away?" Kate asked.

"Mum told Gran," I replied.

"Try not to get so upset," she said.

"But what can I do?" I asked.

"You can talk to your parents and tell them how you feel," she replied.

"I suppose I could say something next time the social worker comes over," I said.

Kate and I went into the kitchen, where Angie was cooking dinner. She had a cauliflower steaming away and was making a cheese sauce to go with it.

"You're welcome to eat with us, Chloe," she

said. "As long as you phone your mum."

I didn't especially like the thought of phoning home, not after what I'd said. I shouldn't have blamed Mum for everything that had happened. That wouldn't change anything – only make her more unhappy.

"My mum has been really upset about everything," I said.

"She has a lot to try and sort out," Angie replied. "She wants you and Ollie to be happy and safe."

"I told her that it was all her fault. I didn't mean to."

"I'm sure she knows that. You were just angry."

"The thing is, I've been feeling like it was all my fault," I said. "I had all these dreams about my natural mum coming for me, then Ollie's dad turned up instead."

"Not exactly like the fairy tale," Kate said.

"No, not really. I wish I'd never let myself think so much about my natural mum. She's not even in my life and I don't especially want her to be."

"There's nothing wrong with thinking things over," Angie said.

I went to the phone and called home.

"Hello," Dad said.

"Hi, it's me. I'm staying at Kate's for dinner – I just wanted to let you know."

There was a short silence.

"Chloe, I don't think you should have said those things to Mum."

"I know. Do you think I should apologise to her right now?"

"No, just go easy."

I felt awkward talking about this on the phone.

"I've got to go," I said. "Bye."

I put down the phone and looked at the others. Angie was grating some extra cheese to go in the sauce. Kate went to get three plates down from the cupboard.

"It's good that you came here when you were trying to get away from Ollie's father," Angie said. "That was quick thinking."

"Did you know what was going on?" Kate asked.

"Sort of, but it all happened so fast. Afterwards, I just felt really faint."

"I remember when my ex-husband, Bill, used to turn up," Angie said. "He was another violent one. I would be in a real state afterwards. I wouldn't feel safe at all. I was afraid he'd suddenly come back again."

"The other night, I was scared to leave my room because I thought that the man would be there."

"It's not surprising after a shock like that," Kate said. "I would have been frightened too. I would have turned on all the lights in the house and probably gone around checking in the cupboards as well. Just to make sure."

"I did end up sleeping on the floor in Ollie's room," I replied.

"Still protecting him," Angie said.

"Now I've got to protect him from my parents and the social worker."

"It's not the same thing. They're just trying to work out what's best for everyone," said Angie.

"Well, they don't have a clue," I said.

After dinner, Kate walked part of the way home with me.

"I'm sorry about everything that's going on," she said. "About Ollie, I mean."

"I might have to run away with him and go and live in the den," I replied.

"I could cycle out every few days and bring you supplies," Kate said.

"It would be perfect," I went on. "I would be away from Mum and Dad. No one would be able to take Ollie away then."

All at once, I had this clear picture in my head. It would be like one of those adventures I used to dream of: Ollie and I would live out in the den, surrounded by fields; I'd spend my time drawing pictures in my sketchbook; we could live on berries picked from the woods...

I knew this wasn't very realistic (I didn't even like eating fruit – let alone a load of poisonous berries). But it still seemed like it could be a lot of fun. First, I'd have to see what my parents were going to do though. If they kept on talking about giving Ollie to another family, then I'd run away. And, this time, I'd go for good.

CHAPTER TWENTY-NINE

The next morning, I lay in bed. I was getting more and more worried. What if Ollie was going to be taken away today? Maybe that was the real reason Jane was coming over: to take him to another family. They'd go off in her car and I'd never see Ollie again.

Maybe I didn't deserve Ollie as my brother. I hadn't been especially nice to him when he first arrived. Then there were all the times when I'd pretended to Mum and Dad that I didn't like him. This could be my punishment.

I got out of bed and paced around my room. I told myself to stop being so ridiculous. Jane was only coming to check on Ollie and he was much better now. She would be pleased. Gran wanted

Ollie to stay and Dad probably did too. I wasn't the only one and Mum would come around in the end. If not, I had my plan to go and live in the den.

Kate had said she'd bring us supplies. It would be a new home without any adults. What more could I want? I wouldn't have Mum and Dad telling me what to do all the time. We'd be completely free for once in our lives. I could teach Ollie how to draw more and I'd get him speaking. I could make him his own set of signs to learn from (without too many rude words).

I saw Jane arrive. She pulled up outside the house and went to the front door. Mum and Dad were chatting with her in the hall. This was my chance. I had to tell them what I thought. I wasn't going to be moody or get angry. Not this time.

I hurried downstairs and put on my best smile.

"Hello, Chloe," Jane said. "You're looking well."

"Hi," I replied.

"How are you?" she asked.

"I'm fine and so is Ollie."

"That's good to hear."

We went into the living-room. Things began to

go wrong when Mum started talking about Ollie.

"What if his biological father comes again?" she said. "He could turn up at any time."

"It is a risk, even though the police say he's not allowed within ten miles of the area," Jane replied.

"He won't take any notice of that when he's drunk," Mum said. "Next time someone could be seriously hurt. It won't be safe for Ollie or Chloe."

"Don't worry about me," I said. "I can cope just fine. I looked after Ollie last time, didn't I? He didn't get hurt."

"You were wonderful," Dad replied. "But Mum's got a point too."

"You could think of some safe places for Chloe and Ollie to go if they ever got in trouble again," Jane said.

"We could go to Kate's house, like last time, or to Gran's," I suggested.

"I don't want you or Ollie to be put in that situation again," Mum told me.

"So you're just going to give him away?" I asked, getting angry.

"No one said anything about that," Dad replied.

"We're just looking at all the options."

"Yeah, right."

"I didn't think you wanted Ollie to live here in the first place," Mum said.

"Well, I like having him here now," I replied.

"Chloe wouldn't have made such an effort to make sure Ollie was safe if she didn't care," Jane pointed out.

"And they have become closer," Dad said.

I was so angry that I could hardly hear what they were saying. I was convinced that I was going to lose Ollie. My parents obviously weren't going to stop it from happening, which meant I would have to.

So much for letting them know how I felt. There was no point in talking any more. I left the living-room and stomped upstairs. I got out my backpack and started stuffing some of my clothes into it. I was going to run away and take Ollie with me to a place where no one could take him away.

I went into Ollie's room. He'd woken up and was standing up in his cot.

"We're going on an adventure," I said.

He jumped up and down, waving his cloth.

"Yes, it's exciting."

I threw some of his things into the bag.

Then I lifted him out of his cot and carried him down the hall. I listened to make sure no one was coming. Jane might have been about to check on Ollie. But I didn't hear anything. They must have still been busy talking.

I tiptoed down the stairs, trying not to step on the creaky bits. The portrait of Great-uncle Herbert had gone to Gran's, so I didn't pass him. Hercules was quietly chewing his teddies in the kitchen. He lay in his basket, watching us from under his wrinkled brow as we headed towards the door.

I hurried around the side of the house and out of the gate. Turning back one last time, I saw Jane and my parents talking in the living-room. I decided to get out of the way in case they could see me too. I needed to reach the country pathway. Only then would we be safe.

CHAPTER THIRTY

I was relieved once we got to the path. We weren't likely to see anyone now. I put Ollie down because I was a little out of breath.

"You're going to have to do some walking too. I can't carry you the whole way."

He reached up to hold my hand.

"We're going to this amazing place," I told him. "An old house in the middle of nowhere. It's a bit run down, but Kate has decorated it with posters and stuff. She's also going to bring us supplies."

I kept on telling Ollie how great it was going to be once we got to the den. I think it was to stop myself from getting afraid. How were we going to cope? There'd only be fields around us. I wasn't even sure if I could look after Ollie by myself.

And then there'd be wild animals. I was likely to get a heart attack at the sight of a grass snake.

I picked up a branch and used it to knock stones off the path. Ollie wanted one too. I searched in the undergrowth for the right size branch and gave it to him.

"There you go," I said.

He ran after the stones I knocked to the side and knocked them back again.

"This isn't meant to be a game," I told him.

But I went along with it.

It seemed to take forever to get there – Ollie really slowed me down. I carried him as much as I could and he walked some of the way too. This wasn't exactly like whizzing along on a bike. The sun was setting by the time we were out of the woods and heading down the hill to the old building.

"Our new home!" I said.

There were sparrows flying around the place. They had nests up in the rafters.

"I think they live here too," I told Ollie.

I checked to see what supplies were already there. There was a packet of ginger snaps left over from my last visit with Kate.

"We should be OK until tomorrow," I told Ollie.

But I was going to miss Dad's cooking. I wondered what was going on at home. Had they noticed we were gone? I remembered the last time I'd run away – my parents hadn't even bothered looking for me. But they might be worried about Ollie this time (though they were planning to send him off to another family anyway).

I opened the packet of biscuits and handed one to Ollie. The sparrows were chattering louder than ever. They swooped down, hoping for some crumbs.

"They're like Hercules," I said, "eating everything."

Ollie kept throwing them pieces of biscuit.

"Don't give them too much or we won't have any left for ourselves."

I didn't even know when Kate was going to bring more supplies. It might not be for days. I counted the number of biscuits we had left: twelve ginger snaps. They weren't even chocolate. Still, it was better than nothing. I looked around the den some more and found half a bottle of flat Coke.

I emptied my backpack and tried to feel at home. But it didn't seem quite right. I'd forgotten to bring any sketch pads and I'd left my watch in the bathroom. I wasn't sure what I would do with my time if I couldn't count down minutes and draw pictures.

Ollie was tired after all the walking. He was ready to go to sleep. I got some jumpers out of my bag and wrapped them around him. I used a cushion as a pillow.

"We could make up a story for you," I said. "It could be a goodnight story."

"O-ry," he echoed.

"Your own story, how about that?"

I tried to think of something.

"Once, there were two children. Well, one of them wasn't exactly a child – she was thirteen. They lived together in an old house next to some woods. They were very happy there, playing with birds and eating biscuits."

Ollie fell asleep, cuddling my arm.

I started to feel frightened as it got dark outside. I kept listening out for every sound and imagining awful things. What if wild animals came in here at night? How would I fight off a vicious fox or a deadly spider? There could even be ghosts here – it was a really old building after all.

The more I thought about it, the worse it got. So I told myself the best thing would be to stop thinking. I needed to get some sleep. I shut my eyes and cuddled close to Ollie.

Then I definitely heard something. It sounded like footsteps in the distance. I got up carefully to avoid waking Ollie and went over to the window to see if anyone was coming towards us. There was only darkness for a while and the outlines of the trees. Then suddenly I made out torchlight and some figures coming along the path.

CHAPTER THIRTY-ONE

The torchlight was coming closer. We had to hide! I woke Ollie up and carried him behind an old wall. I needed to make sure no one could hurt him. It was all up to me again. I wished there wasn't so much pressure on me. I looked out into the darkness. What if Ollie's natural dad was out there? He might have found out where we were. Maybe he'd seen us go up the path earlier.

We should have brought Hercules with us. He would have scared off whoever was out there. He'd have barked and barked. I wasn't sure it was so great now, being miles away from where other people lived. This time I didn't have anywhere to run for help.

I put Ollie down, so we'd be able to hide better.

I crouched low and motioned for Ollie to copy me. Hopefully no one would think of looking for us behind the wall. But then I thought of all our stuff lying around on the floor: the backpack and clothes. I should have hidden them too. But it was too late now.

The footsteps were coming down the hill and into the building.

"They must be here," someone said.

"I hope we haven't come all this way for nothing."

"Why don't you try calling them?"

It was Kate, Dad and Angie. I was so relieved.

"Chloe! Ollie!" Kate called.

"Not too loudly," Dad said. "We don't want this building to fall on our heads."

Angie was shining her torch around the room.

"It looks like people have been living here. In fact, it looks like your room, Kate."

"Not exactly," Kate replied.

Dad shone his torch on my backpack.

"That looks like Chloe's," he said.

I wanted to let them know that we were here. I just wasn't sure how to go about it. I couldn't exactly jump up and wave, saying, "over here". But then they might leave if they didn't see us soon.

"What should we do?" I whispered to Ollie.

He looked up at me with a troubled expression.

"We'll think of something," I said.

But we didn't need to do anything in the end. A torch shone in our direction.

"I've found them!" Dad called.

"Thank goodness," Angie said.

Ollie and I came out. I wiped the dirt off my knees. Dad picked Ollie up.

"So this is where you two monkeys have been hiding," he said.

Kate had this really guilty look on her face.

"I didn't want to tell them you'd be here," she said. "They made me."

"We were all worried sick," Angie added.

"We didn't have a clue where you'd gone," Dad said. "Mum went upstairs to check on Ollie and he'd disappeared. Then she went into your room and there was no sign of you either."

"Usually you don't even notice when I run away," I said.

"You don't normally take Ollie with you and

disappear for hours. Especially after everything that has happened – Mum was in a real state."

"Where is she?" I asked.

"She's waiting with Jane at the house. They wanted to be there in case you went back."

We walked through the woods. Angie and Kate went on ahead. I heard Angie saying, "We mustn't interfere."

Dad carried Ollie, who had fallen asleep against his shoulder.

"Why did you run off?" Dad asked.

"I didn't want you to give Ollie away," I replied.

"Who said anything about that?"

"Mum told Gran the other day."

"I bet you didn't hear the whole conversation," he said.

"No."

"Gran got the wrong end of the stick – just like you I suppose."

"So Mum wants Ollie to stay?" I asked.

"Of course she does. She was upset about what happened – that was all. And she was worried about putting you and Ollie in danger. We never seriously thought about giving Ollie to another family."

"I must have got confused," I replied. "I didn't realize Mum was so worried about me. I was afraid that one day Ollie would suddenly be gone and there'd be nothing I could do about it."

"Next time something is bothering you, try talking to me or Mum. You shouldn't feel like you have to run away. We need to work things out together."

I wondered how Mum would react when she saw us. She'd probably be really cross with me for running off and taking Ollie away. And if Jane was waiting there too, it must be serious.

CHAPTER THIRTY-TWO

As soon as we turned up the path, Mum and Jane came rushing out the front door.

"You found them!" Mum said.

She took Ollie from Dad and hugged me.

"They were out in the middle of nowhere," Dad replied, "hiding in an old building."

"You'd better all come inside and warm up," Jane said.

We went into the kitchen and sat around the table. Hercules was wagging his tail frantically as he nuzzled up against me. It felt good to be back. Mum wasn't even cross. There had been tears in her eyes when she saw us.

"I think the search party needs some hot chocolate," Dad said.

"We certainly do," Angie replied.

I thought I was going to be asked loads of questions. But I wasn't. Dad talked about the adventure they'd had trying to find us.

"I thought Kate was taking us on a wild-goose chase," he said. "It was such a long way."

I slipped out of the kitchen and hurried upstairs to my room. I felt like I was going to cry. Not because I was sad or frustrated – that had passed. There was a lot I needed to let go of. This stuff had been building up in my head for a long time. I crawled under my duvet with a box of tissues.

I thought about when I'd first heard Hercules barking that day and shut him in the living-room. Then that man had come into the house and I hadn't known what to do. I had to stop him from taking Ollie. We'd hidden under the bed. I couldn't forget how withdrawn Ollie had looked, as if he was just an empty shell. And I'd felt like I'd failed him somehow.

I also remembered the things I'd tried telling myself about my natural mum – how she'd take me away from my problems; how she'd be everything my parents were not; how my life would be more glamorous – when really she wanted nothing to do with me. She didn't know who I was or what I wanted. She didn't even know that I'd been thinking about her.

I kept on crying, soaking the tissues. I didn't hear the door open.

"Lo-ee," Ollie said.

I looked out from under my duvet. Ollie was in the doorway, holding his cloth. I wondered if everyone had heard me crying from the kitchen. Or was it only Ollie who knew? He climbed up on the bed beside me and we snuggled under the duvet.

"I suppose we don't need to run away," I said, "not if you can stay here."

A bit later, I went into the bathroom to wash my face. I tried to make my eyes look less red and sore. I wanted to wash all signs of the tears away. I suppose I was afraid to show my true feelings; at the same time, I was afraid no one would guess them. I bumped into Mum in the hallway.

"It's about time Ollie went to bed," she said. She picked him up. "You must be one very tired little boy," she told him.

"He walked a lot today," I said.

"How are you feeling?" Mum asked me.

"A little better," I replied.

Mum carried Ollie into his room and laid him down in the cot.

"You should never think it's all up to you to look after him," she said.

"I thought I was going to lose him," I replied.

"Ollie's not going anywhere."

"You promise?"

Mum nodded.

"I never want to lose either of you," she said, giving me a hug.

CHAPTER THIRTY-THREE

Gran came over for lunch the next day. She brought a hatstand with her; there were about twenty arms sticking out of it.

"What are you doing with that, Gran?" I asked.

"It's a wedding present for your parents," she replied.

"Didn't they get married about eighteen years ago? You're a bit late."

"No, it's a replacement present," she said and turned to them. "I wanted to give you something nice, since I took the portrait of Herbert back."

"Thank you," Dad said.

"Now Chloe and Ollie will have a place to put the hats I knitted them."

"Is it all right for me to hang my hats there

too?" Dad asked.

"I should think so," Gran replied.

Mum smiled. She was pleased to see Gran and Dad getting along for once.

I thought they were going to fall out again when it came to lunch.

"Did you do the cooking, dear?" Gran asked Mum.

"No, it was my husband."

"When my husband was alive, I never let him set foot in the kitchen – not one foot."

"But Dad's a really good cook," I said.

Her hearing aid must not have been working at that moment, because she didn't respond.

"A man's place is in the office, or working outside in the shed."

But Gran changed her tune when Dad opened the oven door. He brought out this delicious lasagne that let off tomato and olive oil scented steam. Gran ate her way through three helpings.

"It looks like you enjoyed that," Mum said, as Gran finished off her last mouthful.

"Yes, it wasn't bad," Gran replied. "I wouldn't mind getting the recipe, in fact."

"So a man's place can be in the kitchen?" I asked.

"If he cooked like that, I'd let him in every now and again."

Ollie was sitting in the high-chair. He'd managed to spread an amazing amount of food around his face. Gran took some tissues from her sleeve and offered them to him. Mum went to get some wet paper towel instead and wiped Ollie's face.

"You're a mucky pup," she said.

"Brothers are important," Gran told me. "I wish Herbert were here today."

"At least you have the portrait hanging in your living-room now," I replied.

"Yes, Herbert likes it there," she said.

The phone started ringing and Mum went to answer it. I wasn't really paying any attention to her, but I noticed how happy she looked when she put the phone back down.

"That was Jane," she said, "with news about Ollie's father. It seems that he's checked himself into a rehab unit over a hundred miles away."

I didn't think the problem was exactly solved.

"He could still show up here," I said.

"There's always going to be a risk of that. But I think it's a risk we're willing to take," Mum replied.

"Chloe has certainly made it clear how she feels," Dad said.

"I definitely want Ollie to stay."

"Well, at least that is one thing we all agree about," Mum said.

"Of course we all agree," Gran replied. "But then I've always been an agreeable person."

"Except for when you're being disagreeable," Dad said quietly.

"We need to be ready in case Ollie's father does show up again," Mum said.

"I could make an escape route in the fence behind my yellow roses – when I get them," Dad offered.

"Great-uncle Herbert is always available to help in times of crisis," Gran said. "He'll be ready to put up another fight."

"I don't think I'll be leaving Ollie and Chloe alone very often," Mum continued.

"I won't have to babysit?" I asked.

"I didn't say that exactly. But I could get a

mobile phone, then you'll be able to reach me more easily."

"I could learn karate, for self-defence," I said.

"Social services will contact us immediately if there's any possibility that Ollie's father has come to the area," Mum said. "If that happens, we could go off on a day trip somewhere."

"I wouldn't mind going too," Gran said. "A nice trip to the seaside would be just the thing."

I thought now would be a good time to slip away. I lifted Ollie out of his high-chair and quietly left the room while the others were still chatting. They hardly noticed us go.

We went upstairs to my room. I got some thick paper out from under the bed. I also searched for the coloured pencils that were scattered around the place.

"I think we should make you a set of your own signs," I said. "We could do some to go up on your door – you're going to need them living around here!"

WHERE I'D LIKE TO BE
by Frances O'Roark Dowell

A ghost saved Maddie's life when she was a baby, her Granny Lane claims, so Maddie must always remember that she is special. But it's hard to feel special when you've spent your life being shunted from one foster family to another. That's why Maddie can't stop looking for a place to call home.

Then a new girl, Murphy, shows up at the children's home where Maddie is now living. Murphy is armed with magical tales about exotic travels, being able to fly and boys who recite poetry to wild horses. Maddie is enchanted and lets her guard down. She shows Murphy her *Book of Houses*, forgetting – though not for long – that she should always protect the things she loves.

By the author of *Dovey Coe*, winner of the Mystery Writers of America Edgar Award.

MISSING PERSONS: THE ROSE QUEEN
by M.E. Rabb

Meet Sam and Sophie – runaway sisters from Queens, New York, who are trying to make new lives for themselves in the tiny town of Venice, Indiana. They've changed their names, dyed their hair ... and even discovered a new talent – finding missing persons. But they must never forget the importance of staying missing themselves...

Case #1:
Missing: Noelle McBride, 16-year-old female, resident of Venice, Indiana.

Physical description: Tall, thin, tanned, frosted blonde hair, nasty expression, tacky dresser, terrible singing voice.

Last seen: Riding in the car of Sam and Sophie.

Comments: The Chief of Police thinks Noelle is dead, and all the evidence points to Sophie. If she and Sam can't find out soon what really happened, they're in big trouble!

CONFESSIONS OF A TEENAGE DRAMA QUEEN
by Dyan Sheldon

Everything I'm about to tell you occurred exactly as I say.

And I don't just mean the stuff about "Deadwood" High, and my fight with Carla Santini over the school play. I mean *everything*. Even the things that seem so totally out of this solar system that you think I *must* have made them up – like crashing the party after Sidartha's farewell concert in New York – they're true too. And nothing's been exaggerated. Not the teeniest, most subatomic bit. It all happened exactly as I'm telling it.

And it starts with the end of the world...